Leviathan Jones and the Sea Witch

By

Michele Beresford

Leviathan Jones and the Sea Witch
Copyright © 2023 by Michele Beresford
Cover Design Copyright © 2023 Converted Books

All Rights Reserved

This is a work of fiction. Names, characters, places, and incidents either are products of the author's imagination or are used fictitiously. Any resemblance to actual events or locales or persons, living or dead, is entirely coincidental.

This work is protected under the US Copyright Act of 1976, its subsequent amendments, and all other applicable international, federal, state, and local laws.

No part of this work may be reproduced, distributed, or transmitted in any form or by any means, including photocopying, recording, or other electronic or mechanical methods, without the prior written permission of the publisher, except in the case of brief quotations embodied in critical reviews and certain other noncommercial uses permitted by copyright law.

To contact the author and for permission requests, contact Converted Books at:
info@convertedbooks.com

Please remember to cite the work (and edition, where appropriate) to which you refer in your request.

Leviathan Jones and the Sea Witch

For Captain Sharktooth Finn of the Great Lake Waters.
You're a scurvy dog but I love you.

<u>One</u>

The night music of Nautilus Castle was changing.

Lev could hear it over the roar of the crashing waves of the ocean outside his window. Old Man Grogan once mentioned to the queen how interesting it was that Lev was often the first to hear the howls of the Ice Wolves. The night's howling marked the arrival of the dangerous pack to the outer fields and meadows surrounding the castle. Lev was also the first to hear them leave as they retreated up the mountain just before spring.

Ice Wolves spent the winter running through the forests of the castle grounds feeding on small game. On the rare occasion, they were also known to attack villagers who strayed too far from the protection of the castle walls and its night watchmen.

Lev's room, high in the tower of Nautilus Castle looked out over the North Sea. While his aunt, Queen Eliza, told guests visiting the castle that Lev's was the room with most beautiful view, Lev discovered it was actually the best place for hearing everything just outside and within the castle. He also quietly knew that it was the only sleeping quarters far from the royal family. He didn't mind though. There were advantages to being alone in a tower far from the others.

Lev knew when the hounds of winter had a particularly good kill by the pack's communal howl. He knew when Brody was returning to the castle after his regular maintenance fitness check with

Grogan. He knew these things long before the watchmen at their guard posts.

Lev listened to the symphony of summer dolphins as they whistled in the shallows and kelp beds that lay between the castle and ocean shelf. Once, when he mentioned how lovely it was to listen to as he drifted off to sleep, the King and Queen looked at him puzzled.

No one seemed to love the sea and all its sounds like Leviathan. For some reason, it made the Queen very uneasy. She would get angry with him and send him to wash pots and pans with the scullery bots when he spoke of the sea. Lev had learned the hard way that if he asked why or what he'd said wrong, she would add time on to his punishment.

The King and Queen were the usual sort of royal family. They lived in a castle. They had guards and the North Sea to protect them. They wore jewels. They had bodyguards (although the bodyguards were specially-made robots thanks to Grogan) and they even had a very spoiled daughter, Princess Amelia. Most of all, they were royalty because like all Kings and Queens, they were hiding a big secret. They did everything they could to hide that secret. This was another thing that Lev learned the hard way.

One day, while scrubbing pots with the scullery bot, Lev began to complain about how unfair it was that he should be punished. "I don't know why my aunt hates the ocean so much. And who cares if she does. It's just because I love the ocean and I'm me and she hates the ocean and she's a powerful queen. It's no fair!"

Bernice, the scullery bot clicked her voice box. "If I tell you a story I heard, will you stop crying," she asked.

Lev thought about this. He finally concluded that a story would make the time pass quicker and agreed, smearing tears and soap across his face with the back of a soggy sleeve.

Bernice began, "Long ago, there were two princesses who lived in Nautilus Castle. One day, Ingrid and her sister, Mariam were summoned to the throne room. Their father, the King declared that his first daughter, Mariam be married off to the king who lived under the sea.

It was no secret that Mariam did not love the sea king who was said to rule with strict laws for his people. In fact, there was a rumor that she, Princess Mariam, loved a commoner. But her father forbade her marrying the common man and instead sent her away to marry the sea king. The second daughter became the Queen of Nautilus and was married to a prince from a nearby country. Thus, Princess Ingrid and Prince Edward became queen and king when the old king died.

Now about the big secret.

One night, when the moon was full, and King Edward and Queen Ingrid were very new to being a King and Queen, the whole kingdom awoke to the sounding of the alarm. It was a night filled with shouts and generals barking orders and arrows drawn and all the things that one must do to protect a castle." Lev stopped scrubbing and listened with interest. He had to give Bernice credit. She was a good storyteller.

"By the time things settled down, a common village man found the problem and presented it to the king and queen. With tears in his eyes, he carried the limp and lifeless body of Princess Mariam and set her gently down on the red carpet before the thrones. Mariam had been found washed ashore and there was nothing to be done. No one could save her.

Queen Ingrid leapt from the throne and wrapped her arms around her sister, sobbing. Just as she looked up to brush the seaweed from Mariam's face, she noticed something moving inside the robes of her sister's cloak. Everyone in the room gasped when they peaked under Mariam's scarf and discovered a tiny monster, wrapped in special clothes that kept him warm. The thing was sleeping. When the monster yawned, gills in his neck opened and flexed. He had spindly tentacles in place of hair and webbing like a fish between his tiny toes.

The next day, a funeral was held with the highest honors for Queen Mariam. Meanwhile, a robot guard was quickly ordered for the monster. No one knew what it might do, you see." Bernice turned to Lev. He had turned white as a sheet. "Oh goodness, lad! It's just a story. It's not real."

Lev clutched the scarf that he always wore and held back more tears. "What happened to the monster?" Lev asked.

The commoner was paid to hide the monster while the rest of the kingdom mourned the loss of their queen's sister. The monster and his robot were hidden away in a cave far from Nautilus Castle. Eventually, the monster grew up and escaped the cave. He returned to the sea and now he lives somewhere in the deep.

"What happened to the robot who guarded the monster?' Lev asked.

"Oh, he died," Bernice said, handing the boy a pot to scrub. "Everyone knows robots rust in the water."

That night, while Lev was sitting on his bed, Brody applied salve to Lev's chapped, red hands. "Brody, am I a sea monster?"

Brody's optic sensors opened wide, and his mouth gaped. "Let's see," Brody tousled Lev's hair as he pretended to examine the strands. "No tendrils here," he announced. He tickled Lev and the boy burst out laughing. "Hmm," Brody said. "You definitely don't sound like a sea monster. Why would you ever ask me that silly question?"

Lev took the scarf from around his neck and pointed to the gills he had kept hidden apart from Brody. His voice cracked as he said, "I heard a story about the sea monster baby who washed up on shore and lived outside of the castle in a cave with his robot guard and--."

Brody interrupted, "Who? Who did you hear that from?!"

Brody was using his stern voice and Lev didn't want to get Bernice in trouble, so he shrugged. "I just heard people talking. You know me. I hear everything I guess."

Brody looked at him. He didn't believe the boy, but he didn't want to make him more upset. Instead, he just spoke softly as he wrapped the scarf back around his charge's neck. "You are the smartest, kindest boy in all of Nautilus and someday you will do great things."

"But the sea monster baby was found on the shore and its mother was dead just like my mother," Lev persisted.

Brody could see that the story had rooted itself in the boy's mind. He searched his mind for something that might help. Why did human children always have their most difficult problems right before bedtime?

"As you know, Grogan created me for you on the morning after you arrived," Brody reminded Lev.

"That's why you're made of spare parts. He made you in a hurry," Lev continued.

"Yes, so I have no memory of before you arrived. Your aunt and uncle have said very little about your past. But even so, here is what I do know. You are kind when the princess is cruel to you. That takes strength. You have learned to read from the bits of things I can steal from the library and the kitchen. That takes smarts. You love the sea and insist on sharing your love of it despite the queen's hatred. That takes courage. Sea monsters are made of many things, but I've never heard of one made of any of that stuff."

Lev thought about it for a minute. Then he looked up at Brody. "You're right I guess."

"You guess?" Brody teased as he tickled Lev once more.

"Okay, okay, you're right. I'm not a sea monster," Lev conceded.

"But you ARE late for bedtime by seven point two three minutes," Brody said.

"Just one story?" Lev pleaded, "I need a good story to get the bad one."

Brody sighed. "Just one. And only if you close your eyes to listen…"

The Mer-song typically arrived sometime in April. (In good years, it began the second week of March.) Lev held his breath as he lay in bed. He strained to hear the hint of melody, the change over from the hungry cries of wolves to the harmonies of the mermaids.

A light hiss from Brody's internal steam combustion chamber interrupted Lev. There was the mechanical click that, even in the dark, Lev knew meant that Brody was opening the shutters from his eyes.

"Do you hear it?" Lev asked.

"No Leviathan," sighed the robot. "Even with my sensors, you are always the first. According to my calculations, the arrival of the Mer-song will be eleven days from now. Nevertheless, I am certain that you will hear it before then. Now go to sleep, young Master. We have a day at the beach with the Princess Amelia tomorrow." Brody's shutters began their descent when Lev stopped him.

"Ugh, I don't want to go," confessed Lev.

The robot expelled steam as he stood from his chair near the window and crossed the room to his charge's bed. He sat by Lev's feet. "Don't be silly," said Brody. "You have loved the beach since the day you arrived. There is not a single thing that you dislike about the place where water meets the shore. In the summer, I must drag you away."

"It's Amelia," sighed Lev. "You know how she is."

Princess Amelia never wasted an opportunity to tell Lev that, even though he lived in the castle, he was not royalty. He was there thanks to the kindness of her royal family. He was an orphan who washed up one night and that was all he would ever be. Furthermore, she often added, he had better be nice to her and give her whatever she wanted. Someday Amelia would be the queen. He should remember that if he wished to remain at court. If he was particularly obedient, she might even let him take care of her horse one day.

Brody cocked his head to one side as Lev pleaded with his protector. But Brody was not an elegant robot. He didn't take kindly to pleading. He followed orders as best as he could. He was clearly made from spare parts. While his outer shell may have been crude, comprised of teaspoons and refurbished toaster ovens, drainage pipes and truck manifolds, his spark, the part that makes one thing alive and another thing not, was kind and loyal. "Would it help if I played the recording we made of last year's Mer-song?"

Secretly, Lev did not want to stay at court, or be a royal subject when he was older. He certainly did not wish to be a stableboy for the rest of his life, nor did he want to give in to every whim of the Princess Amelia. Lev had his own dreams. They were dreams he never told anyone, not even Brody.

"Oh, I guess that will help," Lev sighed. Brody played the haunting melody and Lev lay awake in his bed when he should have been sleeping. He dreamed of a life on a ship at sea where he was part of a crew by day and listening to the Mer-song up close by night. He gave his loyalty to his Captain, not a selfish princess and he went where there was adventure and treasure and battles to be won.

The recording ended. "Shall I play it again" Brody asked.

"Rest easy, my friend," answered Lev. The bodyguard returned to his post and powered down to scanning mode.

Lev breathed in deep, taking in the smell of the ocean as it blew in from his open window. He closed his eyes and listened one last time. For just a moment, he thought he heard the sweetest voice in all the world call his name. "Le-via-than, I brought you a present," said the voice. "Now go to sleep, you silly boy for I shall give it to you in the morning." Lev was suddenly unable to stay awake. His eyes grew heavy but he fought to keep listening.

"Wait," he whispered. "A present? You brought me a present? It's not even my birthday."

"What did you say Leviathan?" Brody asked.

Before he could answer, he was asleep and dreaming of a shining cutlass at his hip as he rode a hoverboard over the waves, chasing a half girl, half fish as they played a game of tag. They were laughing as Brody called to Lev from a giant sailing ship.

He woke the next morning to the same familiar voice. Brody was gently saying his name as the rays of the sun shone faintly on the bedroom walls. Lev rubbed his eyes and recalled the sound of a mermaid singing his name and smiled. It was a good dream.

<u>Two</u>

While Brody was in kitchen at the center of the castle preparing Lev's breakfast, Brody's voice counterpart was fluttering above Lev's head telling him to wake up for the second time that morning. SingSong was a very annoying mutant of sorts, one half children's tea pot shaped like an elephant and one half mechanical bird used in classroom physics experiments. Leviathan had been having the best dream. SingSong had to go and ruin it.

"Go away," Lev moaned.

"*Good morning to you,*

Good morning to you.

Good morning, good morning." He paused for dramatic effect and a big finish. "*Good morning to you,*" crooned the nano bot.

He stared at Leviathan, waiting for applause. His eyes made a clicking noise as they opened and shut. He was rewarded with a scowl whereupon Lev pulled the covers over his head. The little elephant swiveled it's trunk like a propellor and landed at Lev's feet. "Brody wishes to convey his happiest good morning to you. You'd better be down for breakfast soon."

"I got that," snarked Lev.

"Fruit and toast with butter and jam," he started again.

"If you're not up, I'll be back again.

Shorts and flippers, swimming togs.

Hurry up now. Don't take too long."

"Ahhhh," screamed Lev.

SingSong flew out of the open door and down the stairs in a flurry of clicks and pops. Lev listened intently from the refuge of his blankets.

His slightly open door swung open and hit the wall with a crash, this time making Lev sit straight up in his bed. "Get up!" Amelia screamed. "If I have to be up this early to go to the rotten, sandy, itchy, dirty beach then so do you! Get up, snail snot!" Princess Amelia slammed the door as loudly as she had opened it. Lev flopped back in bed and returned to pulling the covers over his head. He listened to the activity in floors below his room.

Queen Eliza was arguing with the King about the need for days at the beach. She said she was worried for the children's safety. The King was saying something about royal blood needing fresh air and his complete confidence in Brody and Camilla. Princess Amelia then jumped at the chance to ask why Leviathan was going at all.

"He certainly hasn't got an ounce of royal blood in him. Why does he have to come?" Amelia whined.

A scolding came from one of the adults, but Lev added a pillow over his head at that point to drown out the conversation. There were downsides to having the ear of the entire castle. If only he could go back to his dream. What had the mermaid said? Something about his birthday?

He tried to imagine himself on a surfboard that could fly over the waves. He'd almost gone back to sleep when the clattering and chirping of SingSong echoed up the stairs. By the time Brody's voice bot had reached his door Leviathan was shouting, "I'm up! I'll be down in a few minutes!"

Lev put on a pair of shorts and an oversized grey t-shirt. He noted that the shorts, which were clearly hand-me-downs from the knight's charity closet, had a large hole in them. He'd ask Brody to sew it after dinner. Lev lifted his scarf from the peg and wrapped it round his neck. He hated how it felt, but the queen had insisted that he keep his gills hidden at the table. He took a deep breath and opened his bedroom door and headed down the long staircase down the dining hall.

Along the hallway, there were portraits of Princess Amelia as a baby. There was another of the princess on her horse. Finally, there was a huge family portrait of Queen Eliza, King James and Princess Amelia that hung over the hearth in the dining hall. Nothing gave a clue that there was a boy, a nephew who lived in the castle.

Lev sat down to breakfast opposite Princess Amelia. When he looked up at her to say good morning, she merely stuck out her tongue. The Queen tapped her egg spoon on the table and gave her daughter a serious look. "Royalty does not stick out their tongue," she advised. Lev couldn't help but give a little smirk.

While the others enjoyed eggs and toast, Brody brought Leviathan a modest bowl of oatmeal with a pot of cream and a dollop of jam. "Sorry Leviathan," said the bodyguard. "Seems we were all out of eggs by the time I got to the kitchen this morning."

Camilla, Princess Amelia's shining gold bodyguard sniffed. "Eggs must be reserved for the health and well-being of royalty."

"Speaking of the Princess and her safety," said Queen Eliza, "be sure that you do not wade out farther than your knees, Amelia. Is that understood? God only knows what monstrosities come from that horrible sea. There could be any sort of disgusting creature lurking just beyond the shallows."

"Yes, mother," Amelia answered in a sickly-sweet voice.

"And Leviathan, I need not remind you that I will not have a repeat of last year's Beach Day," the queen said as she gave Leviathan a deadly glare. "If I hear of any swimming or dares or contests with the Princess, I will see that you are left with nothing but seaweed for your breakfast for a month. Am I clear?"

"Yes, Aunt Eliza," Lev answered. He went to open his mouth to argue that none of last year's trouble had been his idea. Amelia had been the one to dare him, not the other way around. Instead, he felt the calm, steady metal hand of Brody on his shoulder and focused instead on swirling jam into his oatmeal. When the Queen had turned her head to speak to the king, Amelia stuck her tongue out at Lev again.

A thundering of the castle drawbridge stopped breakfast abruptly. Even in the dining hall, they could hear the giant wood beams groan. Soon the echo of what sounded like hundreds of hooves joined the strain of the wood. There were not actually enough horses in all of the kingdom to make that kind of ruckus. It could only mean one thing.

Grogan.

Grogan was one of the few subjects of the kingdom to show up unannounced. He was not afraid of the king and queen like the rest of the kingdom. Lev often wondered how Grogan ever became the King's inventor. Grogan preferred his meetings to be conducted in his workshop on the beach, a good distance away from the castle. Where the castle was a buzzing place filled with trading, politics and citizens, Grogan preferred peace and quiet and time to think and work on his inventions.

Lev heaped oatmeal into his mouth in the hopes that Grogan might include him on some errand instead of having to attend dreaded Beach Day. Lev could hear Grogan riding on his wind walker, a machine made from dozens of rotating joints and beams. Three large, white sails propelled the beast forward with Grogan seated atop. Grogan's long grey hair blew in the offshore breeze. Whenever Grogan rode the wind walker, Lev thought he looked more like a knight riding into battle than an inventor for the castle.

If Grogan had seen fit to make a personal visit, whatever it was must be important. Lev sat as still as he could, hoping he might become invisible. If anyone one was going to be dismissed, he knew he would be the first and he hated to miss a chance at talking with the man.

The inventor was large with wild hair and a greying beard. He walked with confidence, his huge chest and powerful hands carrying something. "Where is the boy," he asked.

The King cleared his throat dramatically. "Is that any way to address your King and Queen?"

Grogan grimaced but kneeled respectfully. "Forgive me your majesty. I don't have time for formalities. I must speak with you and the boy immediately."

Leviathan felt his heart thud hard in his chest. "Leviathan, return to your room," instructed the queen.

"But Grogan just said—," Lev argued.

King James pounded his fist on the table and the entire room fell silent. "You will do as your told, young man. Brody, take your charge."

"Come now, young Master. I'm sure everything will be explained in time." Lev heard Princess Amelia giggle and his face burned with embarrassment as he and Brody began to climb the stairs.

"Then speak," said Queen Eliza when she thought Lev was out of earshot.

"Alone," Grogan said. His gaze fell on Princess Amelia.

There was a long pause. It wasn't every day that one of their subjects made demands on the royal couple. Lev sprinted the rest of the stairs up to his room where he could hear the conversation better. He waited for the sound of guards. Surely, they would whisk Grogan away to the dungeon at any moment.

Instead, he heard, "Camilla," called the Queen. "Please take the Princess Amelia to the music room and summon her violin teacher."

"But mother," Amelia protested, "I'm going to the beach. You heard Father. My royal blood requires it."

"And my royal ears require a considerable amount of practicing of your violin if you are to perform for the Ambassador next month."

Hearing this, Lev couldn't help but laugh. "Even royal blood has to practice their violin," he whispered to himself.

A moment later, when the three adults were left alone Grogan continued, "I need Brody to retrieve Leviathan."

"Just a moment, you don't give the orders," said King James. "You have your private audience. Now what is this all about?"

Brody was listening in Lev's room, and he whirred and steamed with confusion. Lev strained to listen. He placed a hand on Brody's shoulder. "Be still my friend."

"This was left on the front step of my workshop. I found it this morning," Lev heard Grogan say.

There was a gasp from the King and a pounding again of something heavy on the huge dining table. Lev could only guess it was the King's fist. Next, Lev heard the Queen, "I will destroy them all for what they did to my sister."

"Now just a moment," Grogan argued. "No one knows what exactly happened that night. Remember, the night guard found her taking her last breath. I found the boy tucked safely in her cloak."

"I would bet my life that her last words were of that cursed Meridium," the Queen argued. "She died saving her boy from that wretched kingdom and I will never forgive them."

"And still they have never attacked," Grogan countered.

"No, instead, they come thieving in the night, looking for the boy to kidnap. They will never have him. I will send him to live with in the mountain with the Winter Wolves before I let them take him."

"And yet," Grogan reminded her, "you treat the boy like an outcast."

"What do you expect me to do? With those, those—," Queen Eliza struggled to say the word, "gills of his. The citizens would never approve."

"The citizens don't approve, or you don't?" Grogan argued.

"Silence Grogan or the only one you'll be talking to are the rats of the dungeon!" King James countered in defense of his wife.

Leviathan listened from his room.

Grogan had known his mother? She had come from Meridium? Could that mean that maybe he still had a father?

The next voice was that of Queen Eliza. She was calm and Lev knew that was when she was most dangerous. "We will not speak of this in the castle. I will send word when we can speak of it later; perhaps in your workshop."

"I want to speak of it now!" Grogan whispered. "I owe it to Anna. She would not want him treated this way; told he was an orphan, wearing rags, locked in the tower."

The Queen jumped to her feet, but Grogan was faster. He moved quickly for a giant man and put several feet between them. As Lev listened from his room in the tower, angry tears streamed his ruddy face.

Brody reached up to touch Lev's cheek. He raised his palm and with a series of rigid movements of his fingers, a tiny fan extended from a panel at the base of his pinky finger. Warm air blew from it, drying Lev's face. "Do not worry young master. Grogan will know what to do."

"I don't understand any of this. I thought," he paused and swallowed back tears, "I thought they just found me. I thought I belonged to no one."

There was a thundering boom from the drawbridge. The robot and his charge heard as Grogan and his wind walker stormed out of the castle back towards the shore. Lev hoped with all of his heart that Brody was right. He hoped that Grogan would know what to do and have answers to all the questions swirling around in his head, including what was left on Grogan's step.

Voices exploded as Queen Eliza began shouting and King James shouted back, telling her to lower her voice. There were calls out to the guards and then the two of them spoke in whispers. Lev strained to hear but could only make out a word here and there; "Anna would want," "I don't care," "hide him in a cave if we must."

Lev's heart sank and he gripped Brody's hand tight. It was Bernice's story becoming reality. He was the king and queen's sea monster, and they would send him to live in a cave. Heat and rage flushed Lev's cheeks. He jumped from his bed and opened his door, ready to tell them that he refused to go. Instead, Lev and Brody met three armed knights and their swords.

"You will not leave this room by order of the queen," said one particularly large fellow. Lev slammed the door in reply.

When the castle grew quiet, Lev crawled under the covers of his bed. His head swam with images of guards, his Aunt Eliza's angry face, his gills whenever he removed his scarf. Lev fell asleep gladly this time. Maybe he could run away in his sleep. Part of him hoped so.

Sometime in the middle of the night, a buzzing insect flew in from the window and landed on the small table beside the bed. It clicked its wings loudly and chirped. Lev stirred in his sleep and opened one bleary eye. He watched Brody as he walked across the room. The bodyguard had balled his hand into a fist and raised his arm with four clicks, ready to smash the bug. A tiny voice said, "Wait until nightfall. My master will rescue you."

Lev sat up. "You can talk?!"

Brody stopped himself from smashing the bug just long enough to ask, "And who is this Master of yours?"

"Someone's going to rescue me?" Lev asked, excited.

Brody put a metal finger to his mouth as if to tell him to be quiet. He walked over to Lev's door to listen. The guards were still on the other side. Brody and Lev heard the footsteps of a night watchman as well. The heavy steps were followed by the click and turning of the lock from the outside of Lev's door. They were checking to make sure the 'prisoners' were still in their room. At the sound of the lock click, Brody put his hand over the bug and Lev lay in his bed pretending to be asleep.

The knight nodded to Brody and Brody nodded back, putting his finger to his mouth as if to tell the guard to be quiet when he shut the door. The large man gave another nod and gently closed it. There were three clicks of the lock this time.

Brody carefully released the cricket from his grip.

It fluttered its wings as if to check them for functionality after hiding in Brody's heavy metal hand. It cleared its throat but spoke in a mechanical whisper, "Be ready. Bring only what you must. We leave at the call of the Mer-Song."

"Wait, how? Who is your Master?" Lev asked.

"Grogan, of course," said the cricket.

"And how will he get us out of here? The door is locked, and it's a sheer drop to rocks below that window," Brody whispered.

"Master Grogan always knows a way. Just be ready for the journey ahead."

"Where are we going?" Lev asked.

Instead of answering, the bug fluttered its metallic blue wings again and flew out of the window.

<u>Three</u>

Grogan did not come the following day or that evening. He did not come the next day as the sun was sinking into the sea. He did not come when the Night Watchman unlocked Leviathan's bedroom door to let Cook bring in his dinner. Lev spent the last several evenings tracing escape routes in the crumbs of the stale bread and cheese he was brought each day. Brody paced so much that Lev had to pour his thermos of hot tea into the robot's steam chamber.

"I know we are both nervous, Master Leviathan but you really must eat. We do not know when you will do so again."

"Do you really think he'll come?" Lev asked.

Brody sliced the cheese and bread to make a sandwich and inspected it. He handed it to the boy. "Why do they call her Cook if she is not competent to make anything worth eating? I'm sorry Lev. The food I make is better, but you must eat, nevertheless. To answer your question for the seventy-eighth time, Grogan will come. I am certain."

Lev took a bite from his sandwich and looked over at the bags each of them had packed and hidden under Lev's bed. The single candle that Cook had left on that day's platter flickered in the darkening room. Lev's thoughts began to wander.

What if Grogan was caught by the guard on his way to the castle? What if Grogan was already shackled in the dungeons? What if the cricket was just a trick sent by Amelia to give him false hope? What if he and Brody really were stuck in the castle until the Queen decided what to do with them? What would his aunt do? Would she really send him away to live with in a cave like the baby sea monster in the story? Would she answer his questions about his mother and father? Had his mother really known him and tried to protect him? Protect him from what? Terrible images raced through his mind too; Grogan in the dungeon fighting off rats with his boots, Brody turning to rust as they sank into the sea, Lev's own face and hair becoming a grotesque sea monster.

'We leave at the call of the Mer-song,' the insect had said. All they could do was wait and listen. As the days passed, Brody stood guard while Lev fell asleep and woke. There was nothing else to do, no books, little food, not even paper and pencil. Soon, with his water containment unit at half, Brody was forced to sit near the window and power down. On the fifth night, two lay wrapped in darkness with only the light of the moon coming into the window. Their only companions were the occasional tiny spider that had scaled the castle wall and taken refuge on Lev's ledge.

He folded pieces of napkin that Amelia had left that day. Sometimes Amelia wrote nasty notes on them and slipped them under his door. Sometimes she played her violin just outside his door. He couldn't tell if she meant to torture him or cheer him up. Either way it was awful, and she must have known. Soon, the guards on post put a stop to her visits all together. That was at least one good thing about having knight at his door.

One day, Lev and Brody watched from the tower as the royal family went out for a picnic in the meadow. This was the worst kind of day. There was nothing from the castle rooms below to listen to. All they could do was count the strange little spiders who came into Lev's room and then fell asleep (or died, Lev wasn't brave enough to check which.) The strange little spiders had red, glowing eyes and had a shine on their bodies when the sunlight hit them just right. Each day more and more showed up.

Then, on a Sunday morning, just as Cook arrived with yet another loaf of stale bread and a hunk of cheese, one of the little arachnids woke up. Its tiny little eyes watched her from just under the small wooden table. As she turned to leave, it leapt from the floor and on to her tray. The poor woman screamed, and the guard came rushing in. She pointed to the scurrying bug with a trembling finger. The guard rolled his eyes. He picked up the spider and threw it out Lev's window. As soon as the guard left, the bug returned triumphantly on the windowsill.

The next day, a small basket arrived from King James. While Queen Eliza may have been continuing to fume about the strange package left for Lev as well as Grogan's insistence that they speak to him about his parents, King James was beginning to soften. When Lev opened the basket, he found a folded towel. Inside the towel was a honeycomb dripping with honey from the first of spring harvest of the hives. There was no note, but Lev nearly dropped it all when five little spiders crawled out from under the towel.

"Where are they all coming from?" Lev asked.

That night, as he lay in bed, Leviathan heard the Queen complain about the "infestation." Cook mentioned her own experience.

"Tiny little brute scared the life out of me with its beady red eyes. I was sure it would bite me!"

Brody stirred. He went to where a pile of the spiders was sleeping in the corner and picked one up. Brody gave a rare chuckle for such a serious robot and Lev looked at him, puzzled. He set the bug back in its nest and gave Lev a wink. "Won't be long now, young master."

"What won't?" Lev asked.

"I have a feeling you'll see very soon."

That night, sometime when the moon began to climb high in the sky, Lev heard it. He opened his eyes and sat up in his bed just to make sure that he wasn't dreaming. A mermaid was singing. The Mersong was being sung close to shore and Lev felt his stomach leap into his throat. His heartbeat hard in his chest.

Just above the song was another sound that was unfamiliar. It was as if a thousand tiny feet were running through the castle. Tiny metal feet collided with castle stone. Lev listened hard. Maybe it was rain falling on the flagstone outside of the castle. For a moment, Lev thought of the sound of the fire in the great hearth with its crackling and burning logs. He was afraid. Was the castle on fire?

A tiny voice whispered in the dark and Lev gasped. Brody jumped to his feet, but neither could see who was speaking. "Leviathan Jones, Grogan will meet you at the south tower roof. Hurry!"

Lev recognized the voice of the Grogan's messenger cricket. He protested, "Tell Grogan we can't get out. The Queen has locked us in this room and there is a guard at our door and at the top of the stairs."

There was a click and a tiny slice of light flooded Lev's room from the door as it opened ever so slightly. The sound of thousands of little feet was much louder with the door open. "Leviathan," said Brody, sounding alarmed, 'why is the floor moving?"

<u>Four</u>

Lev slipped from his bed and opened the door of his room cautiously. Hanging off the brass lock was a tiny spider with its familiar, glowing red eyes. One of its appendages was swiveling and pivoting on a metal joint. Lev heard the lock inside the keyhole of his door clicking. As his eyes adjusted to the hallway torch light, Lev realized the floor wasn't moving as he and Brody had thought, nor was it raining. There was no fire or smoke. The sound was an army of minuscule spiders. The guard who had been standing at attention hours ago lay slumped at the top of the stairs covered in an army of the tiny, mechanical arachnids.

Every instinct told Lev to run and shut the door before he too was attacked. He had heard correctly when the Queen said the castle was infested. He stood frozen, wide-eyed, his chest heaving with fright. The cricket landed on the doorknob and chirped a command to the spider dangling from the lock. Then, she turned to Lev. "Leviathan Jones, this is your rescue. Follow me!"

Lev snapped to attention with a thunderous boom came from somewhere just outside the castle gates.

"Time to go, young Master!" Brody directed as he grabbed the two bags as well as his young charge.

"But the castle is under attack!" Lev argued.

"That is true, but I think it's our only chance if we ever plan to escape the tower," Brody explained.

Lev gritted his teeth and willed his feet to move towards the castle hall.

The cricket chirped and the spider army made a path just wide enough for Brody and Lev to run. The three zigzagged down the stairs, through the kitchen and to the stairway to the south tower. Guards and Night Watchmen lay sprawled out on the floor at their posts.

"Are they," Lev swallowed hard, "dead?"

"No, no," answered the cricket, "merely sleeping. Now hurry before they wake."

Just as they entered the high tower, a guard came racing down, sword drawn. He stopped for a moment and stared at Brody and Lev. "The castle is under attack! Go back to your room now and lock the door by declaration of the King!"

Two chirps from the cricket and the spiders charged the guard. Lev could feel dozens of cold, metal pinpoints scurry over his feet. It made him shudder. He and Brody watched as hundreds of mechanical legs and feet leapt into the air and landed on the guard. The spiders plunged their sharp, needle-like fangs into the guard's hands and neck. Within a moment, the hulking man was asleep against the tower staircase wall. The arachnid army charged forward with Lev and Brody trailing behind.

The wind whistled through the belfry at the top of the tower. Lev stopped to catch his breath while Brody's eyes clicked and whirred, scanning for Grogan.

"Are you sure this is the correct rendezvous?" Brody asked the cricket.

The sound of thunder boomed again. This time, Lev and his bodyguard could see over the rooftop ledge. There was a steel elephant ramming its head and tusks into the wooden gate. With each immense thrust of the beast, the castle stones shuddered. Lev could feel it under his feet.

Queen Eliza appeared at her balcony and shouted to the shining, metal animal. Lev suddenly noticed that Grogan was standing next to the elephant, shouting commands to it and several other large, iron animals. "Release the boy!" Grogan called up to the Queen.

"No. Now tell your army to retreat and I will ensure that your treason is dealt with swiftly."

Lev heard Grogan laugh. An iron rhino joined the elephant in battering the castle gate. When all eyes were on the two huge beasts, the inventor disappeared into the shadows. Lev's heart sank. Treason. The Queen was accusing Grogan of treason. He didn't blame the man for running. Nevertheless, Lev hoped there might still be a way. Without Grogan there would be no escape. He heard the shutters in Brody's eyes adjust and click, scanning the darkness.

Lev heard the flutter of wings and turned to the cricket. She just smiled as a huge jointed, metal leg stepped over the parapet and on to the landing. The leg, from the tip to the knee, was taller than Brody. The tower floor shook as a second leg, this time appearing right next to Lev, landed with metallic thunder onto the stone. Brody picked Lev up and set the boy behind him, protectively. Two more legs followed and then, riding atop like a wild cowboy in a saddle sat Grogan. The wind whipped through the remains of his straggly hair and beard as the rest was bound to his head by a pair of night vision goggles. The lenses glowed green, making Grogan look like the King of Insects.

The rest of the legs and body of the robotic beast pulled itself onto the tower precipice and Lev reached out to hold on to Brody. Grogan steered the huge scorpion with its curved tail and dagger for a stinger glinted in the half moon light. The cricket chirped and an automatic door opened in the scorpion's belly. The spider army, with their hundreds of legs and glowing red eyes clamored to get inside.

Grogan blew a whistle and a final flying invention arrived; this robot resembled a dragonfly. Its bulging eyes matched the glowing green of Grogan's goggles. It knelt and bowed deeply to Brody and Lev. Neither was quite sure what to do in the chaos. Lev looked back at the tower entrance on the roof. The Queen's guards wouldn't be intimidated for long. A whirring and several clicks sputtered from the dragonfly's mandible. Two seats rose from hidden panels in its underbelly.

Shouts came from within the castle. Lev looked behind him to the only home he'd ever known. "The guards are waking, Master Leviathan," Brody said as he guided the boy into the belly of the dragonfly. "Time to go." Brody joined his charge inside the insect and Grogan's convoy of metal robots lifted off.

Lev felt the heat of flaming arrows fly past his feet. The King's archers were good, but their aim was not true thanks to the venom of Grogan's mechanical spiders. Nevertheless, Brody used his body like a shield to protect Lev, wrapping his arms around the boy as they flew through the air.

"Can we get a bit of cover out here?" Brody yelled to the dragonfly. In response, the two friends felt their seats rise into the small cockpit of the insect's brain. The eyes acted at a windscreen as well as a protective canopy over the top of them.

Grogan's voice came through a speaker in the floor. "Those arrows can't go much farther. We're almost clear. Rendezvous at the Kismet. We will be safe there."

"The what?" Lev asked.

Grogan ignored the question, issuing orders to the dragonfly instead. "Flight pattern Angler 216."

As the dragonfly and steam propelled scorpion made their escape from the castle, they skimmed the coast where the sea met the sand. Lev and Brody felt their machine bank right as it followed Grogan's scorpion out over the open ocean.

"Do you remember when we went fishing on your birthday?" Grogan asked over the intercom.

"I remember it rained but you let me stay anyways. We caught enough fish for dinner that night," Lev said.

The squadron of mechanical bugs flew faster as their wings lit up under the moonlight. The wind current rippled under their wings and for a few glorious moments, Lev felt like he was an actual bird slicing through the starry night sky.

"Do you remember what we used for bait?" Grogan asked.

Lev sat back in his seat and thought about it. He took in a sharp breath as the memory returned to him. His stomach did a small flip as he answered, "Crickets and dragon flies?"

Grogan roared with laughter. "Can you swim little bug?"

"What? Wait!" Lev called back. His eyes searched frantically for a break or a power button. He felt the cockpit jolt and Lev was pushed back hard into his seat. The dragonfly climbed higher and higher into the night sky. Then, just as suddenly, he felt the protective grip of Brody's arm across his shoulders as the robotic insect looped and cut its engines. It pulled its wings tight against its body and the three of them became a torpedo diving straight into the sea. Lev gripped Brody's arms.

He was about to shut his eyes as he braced for the plunge into the sea when suddenly two cloudy white eyes leaped from the water. The eyes were part of a gruesome, snaggle toothed mouth that opened in a split second. Lev screamed as an angler fish widened his mouth and snapped its jaws shut around them.

"Grogan!" Lev screamed. "Help! We've been eaten by a giant fish, not a sea monster, no," his words scrambled in his brain and got caught in his throat. "I mean, I don't know what I mean. Just something ate us!"

<u>Five</u>

Lev was so scared he gripped Brody in silence. In the pitch black, they were sliding down the throat of a monstrous fish. Or were they still in its mouth? Lev wasn't sure. It was an awfully big fish and there was a lot of sliding around. The cockpit shook and Lev shut his eyes this time. Gears and the sound of steam escaping pipes filled the cockpit. He imagined the robotic dragon fly would be crushed by those awful teeth with he and Brody trapped inside.

"Uh, young master, you can open your eyes now," said Brody calmly. Brody's voice was followed by the thunderous laughter of Grogan coming through the intercom.

"How does it feel to escape the Queen and King's archers, Little Bug?" Grogan continued.

"What?" Lev asked, afraid to open his eyes. "I think they're the least of our worries, Grogan. Did you hear me? A MONSTER just ATE us."

"Open your eyes, Leviathan," Brody encouraged with a reassuring hand to the boy's shoulder.

Slowly Lev did as his friend suggested. The dragonfly had turned his eyes into lights. From the safety of its cockpit, the three were floating down a gentle waterslide with a hidden conveyor belt. Lev stared at the vessels and boats, the flying bots like the one he was sitting inside of and all the mechanical animals who scurried about working on any number of things. "Did that fish eat all of these bots?" Lev asked. The inside of the Kismet was one part small boat marina, one part airplane hanger.

Steam released from other large robotic transports which were docked. Lev's eyes widened. The conveyor took them deeper and deeper into the docking bay.

The dragonfly coasted into a slip and was harnessed by a web that brought the bug and its occupants to a gentle stop. A team of androids arrived and opened the cockpit. Brody and Lev were greeted with whoops and cheers and applause. Several of the androids gave Brody pats on the back and one even hugged him.

Lev watched in awe. He had never seen robots act like this. Camilla had spoken to Brody back at the castle, of course. The two worked together to care for their charges. Lev had never seen Camilla show Brody affection and he was sure Brody had never once laughed in her company.

The dragonfly chirped and fluttered his wings, splashing Lev. Lev sputtered. "What's wrong with him?"

"Obviously he's hungry. Rescuing is exhausting, don't you think?" Brody laughed. "Feed him!"

Lev stared at Brody blankly. The dragonfly chirped again and nudged at a box near Lev's feet. Lev opened it to find a treasure of motor oil of various 'flavors.'

Brody broke away from the small crowd gathered at the landing and turned to Lev. "First let's feed the bug, then we should find you your quarters. I suggest the fifty percent synthetic. It's a treat but still a bit healthy." Lev picked up the can. He tossed it to the dragon fly who fluttered its wings to catch it. Lev thought of the castle dogs and how they caught pieces of meat in much the same way.

Brody gave a little laugh. "It's been a long day and an even longer night. You need some food and rest." Before Lev could comment, Brody took Lev's hand and lead the way deeper into the inside of the iron angler fish.

Lev stopped halfway through one hallway. "Brody, we really should find Grogan. I have so many questions."

"I understand Leviathan, but our escape is not over, and Grogan must see to our safety. When we are clear of danger, I am sure that he will come to see you. Until then, food and rest."

When Brody said food, he wasn't kidding. The bodyguard lead Lev to the strangest kitchen he'd ever seen. Instead of a ships galley packed with cans of potatoes and fruit and bread, it was packed with all kinds of odd ingredients. There was axel grease and brake fluid in cans along the shelves. From the ceiling hung coils and springs, buckets of nuts and bolts and screws of every size. Leviathan gulped. He hoped they had just taken a wrong turn.

Brody searched until he found a cabinet marked "Grogan." "Ah," said Brody, "here we go." Inside Grogan the human's cupboard there were fresh loaves of bread and wheels of cheese. There was a copper basket at the back filled with very large eggs. Lev wondered what from what kind of animal they came but was really too hungry to care.

A zippy little bot resembling a hummingbird sped past Lev and hovered in Brody's face. She screeched directly in front of Brody's eyes, "I'm Peck, the Head Chef here aboard the Kismet. Our provisions will be light until we reach Meridium. What can I get your young master?" She was speaking so quickly that Lev had trouble understanding her.

"Thank you, Peck but I prefer to cook for my own charge, if you don't mind" Brody declared.

Peck flitted from one corner of the galley to the other, then back in Brody's face, then in Lev's. She flew around watching as Brody steamed an egg while toasting bread and frying a can of beans he'd found on an extra shelf. The poor little bot clearly did not like other cooks in her kitchen, nor them taking the master's food.

Brody set a huge breakfast down in front of Lev. "It isn't breakfast in the royal kitchen, but it's better than the rations of Cook in the tower."

"It's great Brody," Lev said with a mouthful. "Thank you," he added. It was funny. He hadn't felt very hungry at first, but as soon as he took a few bites, he was suddenly starving. He finished the plate in minutes. Brody looked on with a pleased expression.

"Right and now to your quarters," Brody insisted. With his stomach happily full, Lev had to admit that all he wanted to do was sleep. Brody was right. Brody was always right.

Brody showed Lev to a room down the hall. Once inside, Brody took blankets from a small, overhead compartment and spread them out on an old couch. He turned the table lamp light down. As Lev crawled under the blankets, he looked at Brody, puzzled. "How did you know where everything is in this place?" Brody paused to consider his answer.

"I spent some time aboard the Kismet once before. I don't really remember it. But there are things in my basic programming that were still intact that help me to keep you alive and comfortable."

"You been here before?" Lev asked, surprised. "I thought you were built for me."

"Most of me was," laughed the bodyguard. "Now go to sleep Master Leviathan. It's been a very long night."

For once in his life, Lev didn't argue about going to bed. He closed his eyes and instantly he was asleep. His dreamworld was filled with water, waves, flying mechanical insects and being swallowed whole by a terrible monster of a fish with bulging eyes and a lantern for an antenna.

<u>Six</u>

"Wake up, Leviathan," she said in Mer-Song. "It's time for your birthday present."

Lev shook his head at the beautiful girl with long, floating hair. Behind her, he watched as starfish fell to the ocean floor. "No, it's not. My birthday is in winter."

"You're so silly. Of course, it's your birthday," said the girl. He stared at her, mesmerized as he watched the sun light on her shimmering tail. "Now wake up and see what I've left for you. I'll see you at the party."

"Party?" Lev asked in his dream. She smiled at him and giggled. Then she swam away. "Wait!" Lev called. He reached out his hand for her but instead his hand smacked into cold steel.

"Leviathan," said Brody. "You're dreaming. Wake up." He moved to the back of the room to let the others inside.

"Ow, no. I don't want to wake up," Lev groaned and rubbed his fingers.

Reluctantly, he opened his bleary eyes to a view of shining silver and steel. His couch was surrounded by robots of every size. Lev sat up and was about to ask what was going on, but a chorus of metallic shipmates began to sing.

"Happy Breath-day to you,
Happy Breath-day to you,
Happy Breath-day dear prince,
Happy Breath-day to you."

"Breath-day? Prince?" Leviathan yawned as he rubbed his eyes. He wondered if he was still dreaming.

Peck flitted from the head of the couch to the foot with excitement. She shouted directions as the other robots moved to make room. Brody pushed a cart towards Leviathan.

A burly robot with an intimidating mouth made of recycled saw blades jumped up and down on his shock absorber legs. He clapped his giant hands in excitement. "Fire tower, fire tower," he said in a deep, thunderous voice.

There was a hiss and then the soft sound of a purring flame as Brody held a blow torch to the top of a tiered tower of bolts, nuts, and various pieces of sheet metal. Several tiny wax candles ignited, their light dancing and reflecting off the port window.

"Make a fish!" the burly robot clapped with enthusiasm. "It is the prince's breath-day!"

Brody gave Leviathan a wink. "Make a wish young master and blow out your candles."

Lev stared at his cake of scrap metal and then back at Brody. He wished with all his heart for real cake topped with custard. He was hungry again. He also wished that he understood what was happening. Why were a bunch of strange robots singing him Happy…Breath-day?"

Lev did as Brody instructed and closed his eyes. He made a wish and blew out the candles. "Hooray!" shouted the bots in the room. Peck flew over to the top of the cake and collected the candles. Then, she held up a tiny can of antifreeze. She drizzled it over the bits of bolts and welded hinges. There was another cheer.

Brody intensified his blow torch and cut the tower into pieces. He gave Lev a wicked smile and offered him the first piece. The boy wrinkled his nose and said, "thank you but no." Brody leaned close to Lev and whispered, "I'll make you a real one later."

The two friends looked up to find the very large bot, the one with the saw blade mouth grinning widely at them. He stared at the first piece of cake with anticipation. "Leviathan, this is Geothermal Recycling Underwater Terra-bot. But you can call him Grunt."

"Hello, Grunt," Lev said.

Brody explained, "Grunt makes sure that while we use up our resources on the Kismet, we don't leave any waste to pollute the ocean."

"Hello," said Grunt. "This is my first breath-day party." He clapped his fingers together with excitement as he stared at the cake in Brody's hand.

"If it's your first party," Lev smiled, "then you should have the first piece of cake. Here." Lev passed the slice to Grunt who nearly jumped with happiness as he took it from Lev.

Peck hovered directly in front of Lev's face. Brody cleared his throat and introduced her. "You've already met Peck. She's the ship's cook."

"Hi Peck," said Lev.

"Hello young prince and Happy Breath-day."

Lev cocked his head to one side. "Why do you call it my breath day? Don't you mean my birthday?"

Peck flitted nervously from one side of the bed to the other. "I thought humans celebrated the first day that they take a breath in this world. Do you not?"

"Oh," Lev said, unable to contain a huge smile. "Yes, we do."

"Then," Peck concluded, "it is your breath-day."

"Would you like a piece of cake?" Lev offered.

Peck took a tiny washer drenched in antifreeze and popped it into her long, narrow beak. "Delicious!"

A tapping of metal on cement floor grew closer. The sound traveled from the floor to Lev's bed. It was a slithering, talking bike chain that resembled a snake. The bike chain bot had a Swiss army knife for a tail. For a head, it had two surgical clamps and it had a roll of gauze for a tongue. Lev pulled his covers around him as the creature approached.

"Would you like a piece of cake?" Lev asked as he gulped back fear.

Brody sensed that Lev was afraid and stepped in between the two. "This is the ship's medic, Slice" explained Brody.

"Actually," hissed Slice, "I am the ship's sssssurgeon. My real name is Medicalbot216 but everyone calls me Ssssslice."

"Uh, hi," said Lev, quietly.

"I am a fully rechargeable android and hencccccce, I do not require ssssustenance," hissed Slice. "I just wanted to welcome the new princcccce aboard."

"It's nice to meet you," Lev said politely.

Leviathan breathed a sigh of relief, when Slice turned to speak to Grunt. Brody laughed. "You'll get used to Slice. He might look a bit scary, but he can repair a broken human arm as quickly as he can mend a robotic breast plate. He did some repairs on me when you were sleeping." Brody patted his chest for effect. "Didn't feel a thing."

The rest of the crew came closer to meet Lev. "This is my brother, Astro," said Brody. A tall, humanoid robot rolled forward. Lev noticed that he looked very much like Brody but had round balls at the bottom of his legs where Brody had feet.

Astro gave a little bow and said, "Nice to meet you Lev. Brody told us a lot about you last night. Don't worry, most of it was good." He winked with a loud click of a shutter and elbowed Brody as he teased. "Officially, I'm the ship's Security Officer but really, we all know I'm actually the best dancer in the whole place. Come see me if you want to work on your moves." Astro stepped back and spun around so fast that he was a blur of polished steel. He stopped effortlessly and added, "Oh yeah and you know, I'm the better looking one too. I was really excited when I heard the news that I got to meet my older bro."

Brody didn't laugh.

The door to the cabin opened and Grogan walked in. He seemed like a giant in the small sleeping quarters. "I heard there was a party. Why wasn't I invited?"

"Oh, but ss-sir, you were," Peck stuttered in reply but Grogan raised his hand and kindly reassured her.

"I'm only kidding. I'm sorry I'm late Leviathan. But what's a party without presents?"

For a flash of a second, Lev remembered his dream and the girl with the coal black hair and shimmering tail. He returned to Grogan as he watched the man pull a clamshell out of his pocket. The smooth, pearly white shell was nearly as big as Grogan's hand. He set it down on the couch in front of Lev. "Happy Birthday. This was left on the steps of my laboratory. It must be for you. It has your name on it." Lev looked at the shell. Shimmering in a rainbow of colors was his name. 'Prince Leviathan.'

Lev wanted to ask why everyone was saying he had a different birthday, but he was too curious about the gift in his lap. He pulled the clam shell closer and gently opened it. As the mouth of the shell opened, the familiar Mer-song played like a music box. Everyone in the room made a little sound of surprise. When the shell was completely open, Lev took the contents out. On a cord hung a pendant. "It's an octopus," Lev said.

"It's a Kraken," Grogan corrected him. "And it's your birthright. It is the symbol of your people and your kingdom."

"My what?" Lev shook his head in disbelief.

Grogan nodded. "You are half human; son of a daughter of Nautilus Castle *and* you are also half Mer, son of King Milos and prince of the Kingdom of Meridium."

"I'm a what?!" Lev asked incredulously.

Brody placed a firm hand on Lev's shoulder and then nodded his head. The rest of the robots in the room bowed as well. "That's right young master, you are a prince, and that pendant was with you when you were found on the shore of Nautilus Castle."

Grogan took the pendant and put it around Lev's neck. The large man's eyes sparkled as he looked at Lev with tears in his eyes. "It was your mother's," he said, his voice reduced to a whisper.

Lev pressed the pendant to his heart. "How do you know?"

Grogan heaved a great sigh. "That is a very long story. Most of it isn't my story to tell, not all of it at least." Grogan and Brody sat on the edge of the couch as Lev cradled the pendant in his hand, marveling at it. "But first, I think there was something you asked me to make for you."

Lev looked at him with curiosity. Grogan pulled a large board out from under the bed and sat it on the couch. Lev was speechless. The board itself was smooth, polished wood but at the end was a tiny, steam powered engine. Two wires with metal pads stuck out.

"What are those?" Lev asked.

"Those are receptors. Attach them to your skin as you stand on the board and think of where you want to go. The electricity in your skin will activate the motor."

"Really?" Lev asked, excited to try it out. "That's amazing! Thank you, Grogan."

He jumped up and hugged the huge man. When he looked up, Grogan looked down at him and gave him a small smile. The bearded man had that faraway look that grown-ups get when they're about to tell a kid a story. Lev sat back down and pulled his knees up to his chest as he got ready to listen.

Something caught Grogan's eye and he ran to the port hole window glass. Within seconds, he sprang into action. He reached up to the ceiling and pulled down a bendable, metal tube with a cup at the end. "Status report. Check your starboard side."

"All I see is a bit of floating coral above us, Skipper," replied a chipper deckhand. Grogan let go of the tube returned to the window. He squinted as his keen eyes scanned the dark waters. There was a catch in his throat, and he grabbed the speaker once more. Whispering he gave commands, "Emergency mode. All sound and lights to stealth mode."

There was a scrambling of feet and voices for a brief second and then the ship went completely silent. The luminescent decoy light of the angler fish submarine went dark. All Lev could hear was the faint hum of the engine.

The door to their room opened quietly and the glow from Astro's eyes illuminated the doorway. "Confirmed crossbones, Sir," he whispered.

Grogan nodded.

The entire ship seemed to hold its breath. Engines much louder than the Kismet's passed over the top of them. Astro held up two fingers in front of his eyes to illuminate his estimate. Grogan listened. Leviathan nudged Brody. The boy held up four fingers in the glow of his friend's robotic eyes and Grogan agreed. The Kismet sat silently in the water for a long time even after the ships above had passed.

Finally, Grogan was like a statue that came to life as he stood and put the speaker to his lips once more. "All clear. Stand down but be alert. They're on patrol." Lev heard the click as he shut off the microphone.

"Those were pirates, Leviathan. And I believe they are looking for you. Word has spread quicker than I planned of our little departure from Nautilus Castle." Grogan stormed out the room, taking Astro with him.

"Why are pirates looking for me?" Lev asked Brody.

"Pirates are the sworn enemy of the Kingdom of Meridium. Since you are a prince of Meridium, they will try to kidnap you and ransom you for gold," Brody explained. "While your aunt, Queen Eliza always thought your mother was running away from Meridium and died while making her escape with you, Grogan says the root of the problem was the pirates."

"How do you mean?"

"Grogan is very quiet about the whole thing even though he was there. He agrees that your mother did think you should be with her while she went back to Nautilus, but he thinks that she was attacked by pirates while making her escape."

"If this pendant is my mother's why did someone leave it for me? Who would send me a gift? It's not even my birthday."

"I don't have all the answers, young master. I only know that Grogan believes that you should know who you really are."

<u>Seven</u>

"Dolphin pods!" Grogan's voice bellowed over the loudspeaker, and it echoed throughout the Kismet. Leviathan nearly leaped out of bed in fright. After a long day and even longer night in relative hiding and silence, the Kismet was coming alive once again. "All engines full stop. Let's prepare to enter royal waters."

"Dolphins mean that we're close to Meridium and it's safe to resume ship activity. We've got to get ready." There was a sag in Brody's left shutter and Lev wondered why. He knew that look when Brody was keeping something difficult to himself.

He nevertheless seemed cheerful as he told Lev, "Let's show you how a prince prepares, shall we?"

Lev groaned. "Do I have to take a bath? You know how I hate taking a bath."

Brody laughed. "It's not so bad. I promise. Besides, how else are you going to test your gills after so long?" Lev panicked for a second as he put his fingers to the sides of his throat unconsciously. He hadn't thought about his gills or being under water. He'd never tried it. Did his gills actually work? Could he actually breathe underwater?

Brody led Lev down the hall. The robot's feet clanked on the steel grill of the floor. He opened another door and the two stepped inside. Lev gasped as he looked inside the room. Brody pulled the scarf from around Lev's neck. Lev felt his ears pop and crackle a bit and shook his head at the sensation.

"This room is pressurized to keep the ocean water just at the edge of the belly of the Kismet," Brody explained.

Lev watched the light of the room as it moved in the reflection of the water.

"Are we going for a swim, or do I have to throw you in?" Brody teased.

"Can you…I mean, you're made of metal," Lev asked as Bernice's story still haunted him.

"Last one to the coral reef's a stinking cod," yelled Brody as he ran to the sparkling water and dove in.

Lev hesitated for just a moment at the edge. He felt his gills open and close. Then, Lev dove in after Brody.

The warm salt water rippled through his hair and filled the slits on either side of his neck. At first, it felt like choking. He started to swim back to the Kismet in a panic. Impossibly, Brody was by his side in an instant. "Your body has to remember," his friend instructed. "Just breathe Leviathan."

But that was just it. Everything in Lev's young life had told him to hold his breath whenever water was involved. He had to admit, he could hold his breath longer than anyone in Nautilus Castle but still. Brody held the boy gently and spoke, "Relax, Leviathan. Take a breath through your gills."

Lev's heart raced. He struggled against Brody's grip and tore himself away. Suddenly, the Kismet seemed like a very long swim. Dolphins were chirping and diving, inviting him to play. In fact, they were getting in the way. Lev knew that he couldn't hold his breath and make it back.

He could feel his head getting light. The edges of his vision were beginning to blur. Brody was shouting, "Open your gills Leviathan! Open them!" There was a ringing in Lev's ears. Maybe he would just sleep, he told himself. Brody was shouting. The dolphins were nudging him with their silky soft noses. Desperately, just before he drowned, Leviathan opened his gills and let the water pass through them.

With the steady stream of salt water came a rush of oxygen. It was like remembering a long-lost dream. He had forgotten how to live under the water's surface. Memory flooded his mind and body as oxygen flowed through his system. When his vision began to improve, he saw that Brody was holding on to him. Pods of dolphins were doing flips, encouraging him to wake up and play.

Lev smiled up at Brody. "I'm not dead," he laughed.

"No chance of that happening on my watch," smiled Brody.

"Thank you," Lev sighed. He let himself relax in the water.

Brody's eye shutter opened and closed quickly in a wink. "Of course. It would have been a problem if we'd have come all this way and you had drowned now, wouldn't it? Oh, by the way, breathing isn't all that your body remembered. Look at yourself."

Lev slowly brought his hands up to his face. Webbed skin had grown between his fingers. He leaned in closer to see his reflection on Brody's chest plate. Lev jumped back in surprise. His hair was a dazzling blue and green mixture. His heart was pounding in his chest. While he still had legs, the skin on them had begun to shimmer like scales. His toes also had sprouted webbing.

"This is what your body will do each time it submerges in the ocean," Brody explained. "Well, go on," encouraged the robot. "Test everything out."

Lev had never been swimming. The Queen had given strict instructions that the children should remain on the shore. While Amelia and he had let the waves spill over their bare feet when no one was looking, swimming had never been allowed. Lev wondered if the Queen had known all along what would have happened if Lev had been given permission.

A young dolphin swooped in and flipped. She waved a flipper. Lev waved a hand in reply. She swam a short distance and stopped, looking back and waiting for him. Lev pushed away the water with his hands as he followed his instinct and swam towards her. A game of chase began.

Soon others in the pod as well as Brody were swimming, chasing, and tagging one another. Lev opened his mouth and laughed, gagging on the salty sea water. The dolphins chirped in what Lev understood to be laughing. He had to admit, it was pretty funny.

While his hands were excellent propellors, his legs slowed his progress. Brody patiently waited for him as the pod lead the two to a local kelp forest. The forest reminded Lev of the trees and forests at the base of the mountain back home. This part of the ocean was darker than the open ocean. Sunlight from above had trouble penetrating the thick ribbons of kelp and sea grass. Lev dove under thick branches and swam through the moss colored leaves. They made him shiver when their silky edges drifted over his skin.

Two clicks burst from the dolphins in the lead and the pod scattered. Brody placed his body in front of Lev before the boy could comprehend what was happening. "Elias senses danger," Brody explained.

"What kind of danger?" Lev asked as he listened and searched hard for movement in the forest.

"Sharks," Brody whispered. "They're probably only here to feed like the rest of the fish but you would be something particularly interesting to their sense of curiosity."

"And sense of taste?" Lev asked as he swallowed back fear.

"We're going to just be very careful. Elias has the pod flanking us on both sides. Hold on to my shoulders and don't let go. I think it's best we head back to the Kismet."

Brody guided Lev with stealthy precision. The two swam a few yards and stopped on Elias's signal. Lev learned to listen for the click that meant stop and then for a series of pops that in dolphin language that meant it was safe to move on. They stayed hidden in the swaying ribbons of kelp for a long time while long, sleek shadows passed overhead and to their left. Then, as sunlight returned another click gave the all-clear. Brody moved them out slowly through the clumps of thick seaweed.

Leviathan found it harder and harder to keep still. All he wanted to do was swim quickly. They could see the Kismet some distance away. "I can see it," whispered Lev. "I swim much faster with these," he held up his hands. "Let's make a run for it."

"Those new hands of yours are no match for the deadly speed of a black tip shark. No, Elias knows these waters best. He says that the sharks are rarely ever seen in this forest. Something has drawn them here and they are hunting. We must listen to him and the pod if we're going to get you out of here alive."

And so, they waited…and waited.

It seemed to Lev like an eternity. The sleek shadows of the sharks filled the waters around them. The pod swam in different directions. Some kept watch while others tried to distract the sharks.

"The sharks aren't eating anything," Lev whispered.

"I'm beginning to think they're here for one particular menu item," growled Brody. "Elias and his family are going to need back up. Brody crouched closer to the sea floor and opened the latch to his voice box. His eyes closed as he transmitted his message from his brain to SingSong. Then, he pulled her from his throat and set her wings in motion. Lev wondered if SingSong had ever "flown" through water. He wanted to ask, but Brody had no way of telling him now. The robot sent his voice component in the direction of the Kismet. Lev watched as a tiny trail of bubbles were left in her path as she propelled her way the huge distance between them and the submarine.

She looked so small as she wove her way through the swaying kelp. Then, she was gone. It was funny. Lev had always dreaded SingSong's visits. They meant getting up in the morning, reminders to do chores or warnings to hurry up. He usually detested the sight of her. Now, all he could do was pray that she made it to the Kismet undetected. He hoped to see her again.

<u>Eight</u>

Brody motioned with his hands, pointing to Lev and then pulled the boy down into the thick bed of the sea grass. The sharks were no longer just swimming, they were aggressively on the hunt. Elias clicked several warnings. A few of the young, male dolphins didn't listen and swam up to a couple of the sharks, bumping them hard with their noses. The sharks seemed to ignore them. Crest, one of the dolphins, looped around and headed in for another push. From nowhere, two black tip sharks launched from the kelp beds and propelled themselves straight for him.

Elias fired off a series of commands as the others in the pod went in to help. "Things can't get much worse," Lev said as he watched the fight begin from his hiding place down below.

He gasped and lunged forward to get a better look, but Brody pulled him back down, shaking his head firmly. In that flash second, Lev realized things had gone from bad to worse. Brody pulled Lev backwards until they collided with a wall rock. "Blood in the water," Lev said, his voice trembling with fear.

Brody pointed up. Within minutes of the fight and the blood in the water, swarms of shadows from above them were rushing in. Sharks from reefs and the surrounding kelp beds had smelled a possible meal and came in to see what they could take for themselves.

Lev watched as the sharks blocked the sunlight streaming from the surface of the open ocean.

There was no place to go and no weapon he could use to defend himself. He knew Brody would do all that he could to protect him but how could one robot hold off an entire shiver of sharks?

Lev thought of SingSong. Had she made it? Was help coming? Or were he, Brody, and Elias and the pod on their own. The odds in the fight were definitely not in their favor.

Brody stared down at his hands and body. Lev wished he knew what his friend was thinking. The robot looked all around him. Brody was trying to come up with a plan. He heard Elias send a series of pops and clicks to Brody and it frustrated Lev. Note to self, if he made it out of this alive, he promised himself he would learn to speak dolphin.

Brody shoved Lev behind him hard protectively. Lev held his breath when he saw what Brody must have noticed. Their time had run out. The kelp ribbons were parting fast and Brody braced himself for a fight. Lev put his hand on Brody's back and waiting for the hit.

"I think you left this behind," said a familiar voice. Lev looked up to see Astro holding SingSong in the palm of his hand. Brody gave his brother a slight punch to the shoulder and SingSong made her way back to Brody's speech box. When she was locked in, Brody laughed, "We are awfully glad to see you. Looks like the whole kelp bed is turning red."

"I'm not going to lie," came another voice. "This will not be as much fun as Breath-day cake," said Grunt.

"If you want my adviccccce," said Slice as he slithered through the ribbons, "I would use thissssss asssss quickly assss you can." The snake bot unwrapped his body and gave Lev a familiar-looking board. "Grogan sssssays it will get you back to the Kissssmet sssafely. Jusssst jump on."

"My birthday present!" Lev said happily.

"Hold on a minute. Lev may have a fast exit but there must be fifty sharks out there or more," Body pointed out. "He cannot outrun all of them."

"Grunt will crush," said Grunt.

"I will swwwwwipe," said Slice, extending his scalpel from his tail.

"It's been a long time since Green Beard saw the likes of the Bucketeers," Astro winked at Brody. Brody called out a series of pops through the water. Elias answered.

"Ok. Elias and his family are ready."

"Who's Green Beard?" Lev asked.

"If we make it out of this alive, I'll tell you the best pirate story you've ever heard," Astro said as he set Lev's steam-powered surfboard on the sandy floor.

Everyone looked at Lev. Lev looked skeptical at a flat piece of smooth wood with a steam engine propellor. It was an excellent birthday present. He had rather hoped to try it out for fun, not when he needed it to escape fifty sharks coming for him. Lev played back the directions Grogan had given him. He placed his two feet in the straps on the board and the engine came to life.

Brody groaned. "With all that racket, they're sure to know where we are now."

"Time to rock and roll," Astro said with way more enthusiasm than Lev thought appropriate for heading into a life and death situation. "Lev,

Grogan's instructions are to put your feet in the straps of the board and think of where you want to go."

Leviathan nodded. He remembered. He slid each of his feet into the straps and the board lifted up in a cloud of sand and water. Lev struggled to get his balance.

"The princcciple isssss sssimple," instructed Slice. "Your human anatomy suggestssss that you bend your kneesss."

Through the kelp, a shark tail hit Grunt hard in the back of the head. "Show time," Brody said as he helped Lev straighten up and get his balance. "Grunt leads. Astro and I will clear a path. Follow in our wake, Leviathan. Slice and Elias, bring up the rear and flank whenever you can."

Lev wanted to ask about a hundred questions, but they had all run out of time. Green Beard's thugs had found them. As the friends positioned themselves into formation, a voice rang out through the forest.

"It's not fair. We want to meet the prince too," said the voice that sounded like gravel. A chorus of laughter from the shiver of sharks followed. "Why should the dolphins be the only ones who get to play. Come on prince-y, we're your loyal subjects too." More laughter.

"Don't answer, Leviathan," Brody instructed. "Once we start, no matter what happens, keep going. Go straight to the Kismet." Brody took Lev's shoulders and opened his shutters wide, staring straight into Lev's eyes. "Promise me. No stopping no matter what."

Lev had never seen Brody afraid of anything. He wanted to be honest and say he highly doubted he could go straight anywhere on this board. Instead, looking at his friend he simply nodded. "No stopping. I promise."

Grunt swam first, his fists punching through the dark, green seaweed. Brody and Astro locked their arms side by side. Each had an outer arm for ramming. Brody kicked hard with his metal feet acting like flippers while Astro whispered a command and the balls on his pairs of feet began to spin. Lev stared in amazement. While the two brothers were strong apart, together they formed un underwater battering ram. They launched themselves in Grunt's direction. Lev felt his stomach tighten. It was his turn to go.

He stood up, bent his knees and nothing happened. His heart pounded hard in his chest. While the seaweed still formed a curtain between him and the open ocean, he could hear a fight just outside it's safety. If he didn't move soon, he and Elias and the dolphins would be without the protection of the robotic offense. What was he supposed to do? Oh yes, think of where he wanted to go.

"The Kisssmet," he heard Slice say. "Just think of your room onboard."

A series of images flashed in Lev's mind. Nautilus Castle came to the front first. The board jerked hard left and stopped as Lev's foot slipped from one of the straps. He thought of his mother and the board flipped him completely upside down.

Elias clicked loudly. Lev didn't know what the dolphin was saying but it certainly sounded angry.

Lev closed his eyes and willed the warm ocean water over his gills. He pictured himself, Brody and the rest of his new friends safely inside the Kismet while Grogan welcomed them back. The board sprang to life and Lev opened his eyes only to find his face smacked one after another with kelp strands.

Lev was not prepared for what he saw when he emerged into open water. Sharks were everywhere. Grunt was struggling to clear a path. He would hit two only for two more to replace them in a swirling mass of fins and teeth. Brody and Astro were still working together as a team. Their feet helping them maneuver through the chaos as they too fought off the pirate sharks from Green Beard's crew. A huge shark with a scar across his snout was barking orders as the battle intensified.

Elias and his pod nudged Lev who has stopped to gape. The Kismet was possible to reach if they swam a wide perimeter AND if the robots kept the pirates' attention. The board hesitated. Part of Lev wanted to jump in and help his friends. How could he leave Brody?

He regretted that he'd made his friend a promised. He closed his eyes and thought of the Kismet again. The board sped off and Lev followed as Elias took the lead. Members of the pod swam on either side of Lev. The group moved quickly around the bedlam of fin to fist fighting when a voice shouted in giant bubbles again over all the noise.

"Now there's a prize if I ever laid me eye on it. Fifty gold pieces to the first shark to bring the prince to the surface alive."

Elias' clicks became frantic. Every shark within twenty feet of Lev broke off their fight with a robot and headed in Lev and the dolphin pod's direction. One by one the dolphins blocked attacks from the left and right. Soon, they too were in a desperate fight. Lev saw the shadow of a huge, great white shark pass over him and he willed the board to go faster. The Kismet was only a few yards away.

Lev could see the dark shadow heading towards him and screamed when he realized it was no shadow after all. It was Green Beard's first mate, Razor, and he was headed straight for the bay door where Lev needed to go to enter the Kismet.

Then, several things happened at once. From the surface above, a canon was launched directly into the fight. Lev heard Brody cry out. Above the shouts and calls for help from the others on both sides, Lev listened for Brody and Astro. There was a sickening sound of breaking metal on metal.

Lev was so afraid for his lifelong friend that he nearly forgot about Razor. "I've got something every prince needs. All he has to do is come aboard with me. Think of it as your welcome gift," said Razor from somewhere below him. The sound bubbles floated up and burst with his evil laugh. Then, the threats stopped suddenly. There wasn't time to figure out where Razor was or what trick was up his sleeve. Lev had to focus.

"Get to the ship," Lev told himself. "We need more help."

It took all of Lev's concentration to make the board return to the Kismet. He could hear the fight behind him. All he wanted to do was find Brody. What was happening to the rest of his friends? He was more afraid of what he couldn't hear; Brody had gone silent after the sound of the canon colliding with something.

Lev sped into the bay door and up into the pressurized room. "Grogan!" Lev screamed. "Help! We need help!"

A crowd of robots were doing something when Lev brought his board to a skidding halt. Grogan left the group and ran to the boy. "I know. I know. We'll get him back," Grogan reassured Lev.

"Get him back? Get who back? Listen Brody's been hit. I think he was hit by a canon."

"He's been more than hit," Grogan growled. "Green Beard has taken him aboard the Graveyard." Thundering booms echoed in the pressurized chamber and Grogan grunted. "Green Beard thinks that I'll trade Brody in exchange for you." The huge man gave a wry smile. "Wait until he finds out I've got his first mate."

Lev looked to the source of the thunder to watch as a large mechanic bot with a boom arm was lowering a cage with Razor inside of it. The giant fish was thrashing his body against the bars making the cage swing violently. "Green Beard won't go far without Razor."

"What makes you think Razor is more important than me?" Lev asked in barely a whisper. The thought of Brody made a prisoner, injured or worse on the Graveyard made his heart jump into his throat.

"The Graveyard is an interesting ship. It's powered by fear. While many of the crew members are afraid of Green Beard, it's Razor, a fifteen foot, walking, talking great white shark who'd just as soon eat you as speak to you who actually powers the ship. The crew is terrified of him. Green Beard knows it."

Peck flew in and flitted nervously, bobbing and flying in erratic bursts, "Sir, the Graveyard is hailing us. What should I tell them?"

Grogan led Leviathan to the hall outside where the hummingbird bot followed. They arrived at the large, docking bay where Grogan patted the nose of the dragonfly transport in which Lev and Brody had arrived.

"Sir?" Peck repeated.

Lev and Peck stared at Grogan. "Tell him that you're only the ship's cook and you will find your Captain who will be with him momentarily."

Grogan smiled at Lev. "In the meantime, let's see if we can teach a bug to be a fish."

<u>Nine</u>

"Wait! Where am I going? I can't drive this thing!" Lev protested as Grogan hurried the boy into the cockpit of the dragonfly transport bot. The large man handed Lev a scroll of paper fastened with a wax seal. From around his neck, Grogan pulled an amulet off and gave it to Lev. Lev stared down at it and touched the one that had been his mother's that he now wore. "They match," Lev said, looking up to Grogan for an answer.

"Indeed, they do. Give that to the king so he knows that it is me who is sending you. He won't question that amulet or what I have to say in the message. That's my seal. And Lev, be careful. The king is not known for his compassionate side. If he has been calling for you, then he feels it's time for the two of you to meet. But a king is powerful. Don't say too much. Listen to what he has to offer. Then send a message through the Dragonfly. She will know her way home."

"I can't go meet the King alone. I don't even know how to get to Meridium," argued Lev.

The cockpit shook slightly as Astro jumped into the driver's seat, appearing as if out of nowhere. "I do. I can get us there." The bot looked up at Grogan as if asking for permission before returning to flipping switches and turning nobs. "If my brother can't take him, you know he'd want me to do it." Astro looked up again at his creator, "It's what Brody would want. Someone must keep the prince safe."

Grogan grunted as he considered the idea. "What about that arm of yours?"

Astro raised his arm and flexed four fingers. "I'm only missing a finger. The supply room ran out. But otherwise, I'm as good as new thanks to Slice."

Grogan grunted approval with reluctance. Then, took one last look at Lev and Astro and shut the cockpit tight. "Get him safely to his father," Grogan ordered Astro.

"I will. You just bring my brother home," Astro replied. Grogan gave a wide smile and a thumbs up before banging his fist on the outer shell of the dragonfly. Lev felt his stomach tense as the craft lunged forward, building up steam and pressure to launch out of the Kismet.

The lights of the angler fish vessel quickly switched from blue to red. Grogan shouted out orders and a voice came over a loudspeaker as Lev and Astro grew nearer to launch. 'Engine one failure detected,' came the announcement.

"What does that mean?" Lev asked in a panic.

Astro hit the launch button and the pair were jettisoned by way of steam power out into the ocean. "It means that it will take at least a day for Sparks to find a missing a small finger lodged deep in the cogs of the engine of the Kismet." Astro flexed his raised hand and waived with one missing digit. "Which means we have twenty-four hours to get help to rescue Brody."

"I thought Grogan was going to trade Razor for Brody," Lev said.

"Everyone knows that Green Beard never negotiates. He'll convince Grogan that this time is different and then somehow take over the Kismet if they think you're still aboard."

"Take me back! Grogan needs me! Brody needs me!" Lev shouted.

"Wrong!" Astro argued. "If we're going to save Brody and the Kismet, we don't need one boy prince. We need an army, and we only have twenty-four hours to gather one together."

"How are we going to do that?"

"I don't know, but together we'll think of something."

<u>Ten</u>

"Why don't we just go ask the king…er… my father for help?" Lev asked. "I'm sure that's what Grogan wants us to do."

Astro sighed. "Grogan wants me to get you to the king. Yes. But he knows the king will not help us rescue Brody."

"What? Why not? Why am I going at all?"

Astro was silent for a few minutes and then said, "Do you know why Grogan has an amulet that matches your mothers?"

"No," answered Lev.

"A long time ago, when Grogan and your mother were young, they fell in love even though they knew that she was promised to your father, King Milos. Your mother begged to be released from the engagement to marry Grogan instead, but her father refused.

After she was sent to Meridium and married King Milos, it was rumored that she was very unhappy. King Milos was wealthy, but he did not love his queen. It is said that she would walk the castle at night because her broken heart would not let her sleep. One night, she saw a knight wearing a medallion like the one you're wearing. It was the Knights of Mer symbol. Anyone who wears that medallion has free, safe passage in and out of the Kingdom of Meridium. Your father gave the one you're wearing to your mother on the day of their wedding, but she didn't know, at the time what it meant. No one knows how your mother had a second one made. Some say the knights themselves felt sorry for your kind mother and made it for her.

But Grogan used the second one she gave him to come in through the kingdom gates to see her in secret. That's how they say it happened…."

"What happened?" Lev asked.

"No one knows for sure but there are stories. One says that Grogan and two of his robots snuck into the kingdom with Grogan's medallion. He'd brought the bots to keep watch while he and your mother spent time together at a secret location. One of the bots malfunctioned. Maybe it was the sea water, maybe it was the pressure of the deep, no one knows. The robot shut down. He failed to report to Grogan that they had been followed."

"The king's guards followed them?" Lev asked.

"No. Green Beard. The pirate had been looking for a way in to Meridium for years. He and a small crew lead by Razor snuck in and stole a large portion to the kingdom's treasure. They would have stolen all of it if it hadn't been for the loyal second bot who discovered what had happened and warned Grogan and your mother."

"Grogan called in his tiny army of spider bots who stopped Green Beard from plundering the entire Treasure of the Kraken. Nevertheless, it woke the entire kingdom and even though Grogan had saved the kingdom from being ruined by Green Beard and his pirates, it was he and Queen Anna's secret that had led to the treasure's discovery in the first place."

"Is that why my mother ran away with me? Was the king going to punish her?"

"No one knows. Did she run back to Nautilus Castle to get away from King Milos? According to Brody, the answer is no."

"Brody knew my mother?"

"A version of Brody knew her and protected her and loved her as much as he loves you now. You see, Brody was found in pieces shielding you and her when they found you on the beach. Grogan rebuilt him from spare parts in his workshop so that some part of your mother, her protector would always be with you."

Tears welled in Lev's eyes as he thought of Brody in the clutches of Green Beard. His stomach flipped with he thought of what the pirates might do to his best friend. Lev asked, "Do you think the stories are true? Do you think she ran away from my father?"

"I don't know," Astro answered honestly. "I am only sure of two things. First, the mermaids have been singing to you, calling you home since you arrived on land. That seems to me like your father wants to have you return to the kingdom."

"And the second?"

"The second thing I know is that all robots and humans are banned from the kingdom of Meridium."

"But I'm human and you're a robot! Is Grogan crazy?" Lev said, alarmed.

"You're half human and half Mer. You are also of royal blood, born under the water and you have the gills to prove it. And that's why I need you to sing."

"Sing?" Lev questioned.

"If the mermaids have been singing to you, then someone wants you home. There is a small chance that maybe…just *maybe*…those Mermaids were not sent by the King. I'd like to see before we get any closer to the kingdom. I can't help you once you're *in* Meridium. But I can help you outside of it."

"I don't understand," Lev said, frustrated.

"Grogan thinks your father, the king wants you to come home. What if the singing wasn't sent from the king? I mean, if a king wanted his son home, wouldn't he send a messenger to Queen Eliza?"

Lev thought about that for a minute.

Astro continued. "I think someone else has been calling you home. It's just my own theory and what does a bot know? But I'd like to test it out before we enter royal waters."

"Who else would call me home?"

"I don't know. Maybe it's someone who knew your mother or you. The kingdom of Meridium is very secretive. No one who lives outside of it knows very much about what happens inside of its walls."

"And you want me to sing?" Lev asked, still questioning Astro's plan.

"While we are still a good distance from the kingdom, I want you to sing the song that someone has been singing to you since you were a baby. Let's see who answers and if they are willing to gather some fighters together to join us against Green Beard."

"And it if is my father, the king?" Lev asked.

"If the king answers, then you're on your own once you step foot inside of Meridium. I will not be permitted to enter."

Lev felt the knot in his stomach twist when he thought of meeting the king. He didn't like the idea of going into Meridium alone. Lev had always had Brody with him.

It was nice to think that he wasn't an orphan though. Lev had always wanted a real family. The idea of having a father was tempting. But could he love someone who didn't ever permit Brody or Astro from entering the kingdom?

Lev swallowed hard at the possibility that he would never see Brody again. Even if they rescued Brody somehow. Where could they go? Was there a place on land or under the sea that would accept a half human, half mer prince and a robot?

Astro interrupted Lev's thoughts. "Grunt and Peck have the team on standby. They'll protect Grogan as long as they can. But you saw Razor and his sharks. We can't beat them and save Brody without help."

Lev knew Astro was right. He took a deep breath. "Can you find a place to hide her?" Lev gestured to the dragonfly transport. "I think I need to be in the water to reach them.

"You got it!" Astro beamed. "There's an ocean shelf just over this ridge. We can hide behind some coral."

'Great,' thought Lev. 'Now all I have to do it get back in the water, open my gills and remember the words." His heart thudded hard in this chest at the thought. 'Think of Brody,' he told himself.

<u>Eleven</u>

It was different this time. Lev waited for the cockpit of the dragonfly to lift. Water flooded the inside in an instant. This time, Lev wasn't afraid of drowning. He had complete faith in his gills. The water was now his second home. The dragonfly chirped happily as if the water washing through its controls tickled. Astro swam to the ridge just over the ledge to keep guard. Lev instantly felt his breathing shift from lungs with air to gills filled with water from the sea.

The scales on his legs raised up from his skin. Webbing grew from between his fingers and toes. If he'd had a mirror, he knew that his hair would be the color of aquamarine and algae. He swam to Astro when the metamorphosis was complete. Together they looked out over the coral ridge out into the deep blue. Meridium was out there, somewhere. Lev wasn't entirely sure how far.

"Do you really think anyone will hear me?" Lev asked.

"This ridge is just out of the sonic range of known Meridium sentries. We're far out but not too far. If someone can hear you, let's hope they'll be listening just a bit better than the royal guard."

Lev thought it was very unlikely he would get a response and he wondered if he should be wasting his time with Brody's life at stake. Then again, he didn't have any better ideas. "Here goes nothing." Lev closed his eyes. He'd heard the song so many times he was sure that it was long in his memory. Yet, when it came time for him to sing, he couldn't be certain he knew the words. He realized he'd never spoken the Mer language, let alone sung it. What if he wasn't singing some version of "Happy Birthday" but rather a song more like King James's soldiers sang as they headed into battle? How could he be sure he was saying hello and not declaring war?

Lev thought instead of Brody. If his best friend were here, what would he say? Lev held that thought and opened his mouth.

Singing under water is much different than singing on land. Lev closed his eyes as he remembered the song and bubbles tumbled out of his mouth. The bubbles were filled with words, and they floated away from his lips and out, into the vast ocean. The air pockets filled with sound jiggled like jelly in the moving current of water. Lev opened his eyes and watched them in fascination as he sang the song again.

Astro's optical shutters spun as he strained to keep an eye on the bubbles' journey towards the outskirts of Meridium. When they were completely out of sight, he turned to Lev. "And now we wait," he said.

If the singing had been difficult, the waiting was impossible. A thousand fears ran through Lev's mind. Most of all, he wondered about Brody. Was his best friend ok? Had Grogan managed to trade Razor for Brody yet? Astro didn't think so.

At least they weren't alone. The ridge had a healthy coral reef that supported all kinds of colorful fish and crustaceans. He was fascinated by the inhabitants of the colorful system. The hustle and bustle of the entire reef reminded Lev of the village of Nautilus Castle. Tiny fish hid in the shelter of the coral while larger fish fought for their place higher up in the food chain. Schools of fish found safety in numbers and protected the reef like the king's soldiers. An eel swam over a tall coral, taking in his surroundings. When he glanced out towards the rocky shelf, he noticed Lev and froze. An electric pulse spread through the water of the coral issuing a message that brought the entire mini, underwater city to a stop. Dozens of eyes gaped at Lev. Finally, the eel bowed his head. A bubble tumbled from its mouth. When it reached Lev's ear, he heard the words, "My Prince."

The other fish followed in the eel's example. Heads bowed and fins lowered show respect to the long lost prince. Astro stared in wonder as Lev swallowed hard. He didn't know what to do or say. No one had ever bowed to him before. He had always just been 'the queen's nephew' and nothing more. Lev thought of Brody again and what he had said about Lev's colorful appearance when he had first changed. His scales and hair were the mark of royalty.

Lev raised his hands and tried to smile. "Thank you, but really there's no need for all of that," he said, dozens of bubbles tumbling out towards the reef.

Meanwhile, Astro watched as hundreds of bubbles rose from the gathering schools and traveled out towards the kingdom and open sea. "Time to move," he said. "I'm not sure how fast word travels by sea but I have the feeling the king will know of his son's arrival pretty quickly. The entire reef is talking about you." He pointed to the stream of messages making their way towards Meridium.

The two swam hard to the dragonfly transport bot hiding in the ridge. They climbed aboard, Astro hurriedly flipping levers and switches as the glass cockpit shield lowered slowly. Lev was fastening a harness over his scaly shoulders when one small bubble made its way inside and floated up to his face and shimmered there. Without thinking, he popped it with his finger and heard a loud plead. "Wait!"

Astro wasn't paying attention. "We don't have time to wait," he said, preparing the cockpit to expel it's water.

"I didn't say that," Lev explained. He gripped Astro's shoulder and pointed to the front of the transport. "She did."

Floating before them wasn't just any girl, it was THE GIRL; the one from his dreams, the one who had left him his birthday gift. A sigh of relief escaped his gills. Until this moment, he hadn't realized just how much he had hoped he would find her or rather, she find him outside of the realm of dreams. They stared at each other for a long moment.

She motioned with her hands to come with her. Lev saw more bubbles escape her lips, but they hit the glass of the cockpit window outside of the dragonfly and he couldn't make out what she was saying.

"Tell her to get in. We can talk on the way," Astro instructed, a bit impatiently.

But before Lev could tell her, she was swimming away from the reef. "Stop!" Lev shouted as he hit the button to raise the cockpit glass once more.

As soon as there was enough room to squeeze, Lev swam hard to catch up to her. "Wait!" he shouted. "You don't understand. We have to get out of here. I," he paused. "I want time to talk to you. But the king will know I'm here by now. I have so many questions I want to ask you before I go to Meridium."

She smiled and stopped to take his hand. "Come with me. I know a place."

"But my friends," Lev hesitated and pointed to Astro and the dragonfly.

"They can come too. Hurry."

"My name is Lev, by the way. It's Leviathan, actually," he corrected himself.

"I know, silly. I've been singing to you since I was a little girl." They made their way over a large section of coral and found where the reef met the ridge. "You can leave your transport here. My friends in the village will keep her safe. Now, come with me."

Astro and Lev followed the girl down, down into the deep waters following the ridge to it's base. There, hidden in the darkness was a wall of seaweed. She swam through it and the two friends followed her. Lev was shocked to find himself inside of a house hidden by a curtain of weeds and built into the rock of the ridge. In one hundred years, he never would have known it was there.

The girl swam to an older woman and hugged her. The woman cooked on tiny volcanic cones that poked out from the floor in the corner of the kitchen. The mermaid turned and smiled at Lev.

"I am Ezra and this is my mother," she said. "Welcome to our home."

"I am Leviathan and this is my friend Astro," he pointed to the robot beside him. "Your home is amazing."

"Thank you," she gave a slight bow. "We know who you are, young prince" said Ezra's mother. "You may call me, Maurea."

"Maurea," repeated Lev.

"I was in the service of your mother when you were born. I was her assistant."

"You knew my mother?!" Lev asked, excitedly. "You really knew her? What was she like?"

Maurea laughed but her expression was one of pity for a boy who never knew his mother. "She was a lovely woman. Sad, but lovely. The only time I saw her truly happy was when she was with you."

Lev swallowed the lump that had suddenly formed in the back of his throat. "She was sad?" He'd heard the story from Astro that his mother loved Grogan and not King Milos but he hadn't imagined how she would be in an average day.

Maurea took a shell-shaped pot off of the volcano vent and poured a thick liquid into several small saucers. To his surprise, the liquid did not float away. She brought a tray of them to the table. Unsure of what to do after Maurea gave him a serving, Lev watched as Ezra as she slurped from her own saucer. Lev followed her example. The liquid was thick and tasted like warm broth. His stomach rumbled for more and he blushed with embarrassment. Without a word, Maurea sat another saucer in front of Lev and he hungrily slurped up a second helping.

"I don't mean to be rude," Astro interrupted, "but Green Beard has taken my brother and we either need to get help here on the outskirts of Meridium or Lev has to present himself to the king and ask for the help of the army."

Maurea sniffed. "You will never get the help of King Milos."

""Why?" Lev asked.

"King Milos thinks that Queen Anna betrayed him with the help of your metal men. He would never send an army to rescue a robot. He thinks he lost much of the kingdom's gold because of Grogan's robotic guards. King Milos is an angry and cruel man. It has always been his way. His people suffered under his rule before Queen Anna arrived and they suffer even more now that he grows old and alone. We had hoped that marrying a kind princess would melt the ice from his heart. Instead, with every passing year he grows worse."

"Grogan thinks that King Milos has been calling me," Lev said.

Maurea hugged her daughter. "We have been calling you, hoping that the kindness of Queen Anna was passed on to her son. That is why many of King Milos's subjects, like us have moved outside of the safety of the castle walls. Better to take our chances with pirates than suffer under the hand of a tyrant. We wait for a time when a new King will bring peace to our ocean."

Ezra slurped her soup. She wiped her mouth with the back of her hand and said, "That's why I've been singing to you. I mean, we need a new king and you're a prince."

"I'm just a kid," Lev argued.

"You found your way this far," she countered.

Astro laughed and held up a hand as if to say he was sorry. "I don't think King Milos is going to give up his throne so easily."

Ezra shrugged. "Queen Anna always said her son would be great king some day."

Lev stared at Ezra. All this time it had been her singing to him on his birthday. Astro tapped a metal finger on the table and Lev blinked away his thoughts. Time was growing short.

"All I know is that I need help to rescue Brody. We can't go up against Green Beard and his pirates with a few of Grogan's spider bots and a small number of robotic crew members. Do you think anyone here can help us?" Lev asked.

Maurea's eyes widened. "Grogan is with you?"

"He brought me here. Well, kind of. It's a long story but he thought King Milos was sending the mer-song. He thought the king wanted me to come home."

In that moment, Lev was grateful that Astro had suggested returning the message of the mer-song. What would have happened if he had gone to meet his father first? He really was clever, just like Brody.

Ezra looked serious when she said to Lev, "Your people need you."

Maurea added, "Here, we are just kelp farmers and fish ranchers. No fighters live here. King Milos rounded up any men or women with the skills for soldiering and forced them into his army a few years ago. If you really want help to get your friend back, you will need the guile and stealth of Madame Haaf and her Sea Snakes."

Lev shuddered. He didn't really like snakes and the thought of warrior, underwater ones sounded like the last thing he would ever need in his life. He tried to hide his fear from Ezra though. Instead, he looked up at Astro. "What do you think?"

"How far are these fighting snakes?" Astro asked. "Can we get there by transport?"

"Of course. It would be just a couple of hours by way of your dragonfly," Maurea said.

"Once we are there, we will need a way to convince them to help us. Who is this Madame Haaf?" Astro sighed.

"You are in luck," Maurea smiled. "The Sea Snakes are the loyal pets of Madame Haaf. She is an enchantress and witch. I knew her a long time ago."

"Why does visiting a witch and her fighting snakes sound like the opposite of being in luck?" Astro asked.

"Because," Maurea said, "Madame Haaf was friends with Queen Anna while she lived in the palace. It is said that the Enchantress helped the queen when the prince was born. I was the queen's assistant but I was not allowed in the birth chamber. Madame Haas was the royal healer at the time. She is said to have had a gift for the young prince but Queen Anna left the kingdom before she could give it to him."

Maurea turned to Lev, "Show her your mother's medallion that you wear around your neck. See what gift she has for you. Perhaps you can convince her to help you claim your friend's freedom. Beware, the snakes patrol her ship at the bottom of the sea. Offer them a gift and be respectful or they will shred you to pieces before you ever see the Witch."

"This birthday of yours just keeps getting better and better," Astro groaned. "Where can we find this Enchantress?"

"King Milos accused Madame Haaf of helping Queen Anna escape and banished her from the kingdom. She lives on the ocean floor near Ship Wreck Alley," Maurea instructed. She took a large piece of flat seaweed from a shelf in the kitchen and drew a simple map.

"Thank you…for the map, for the food," Lev said to Maurea. "And the information about my mother." He turned to Ezra, "and the singing. It was….nice." He smiled at her and she smiled back.

<u>Twelve</u>

Maurea and Ezra waved from just outside of the dragonfly bot. They had supplied Lev and Astro with a few shells full of soup and rough directions on how to get to the lair of the Enchantress. They had promised to try to find as many farmers and supporters of the prince to help them fight Green Beard while Astro and Leviathan were away.

Lev checked the clock inside the cockpit. They only had fourteen hours left. His stomach sank as he thought about Brody and what might be happening between Grogan and Green Beard. "We have to hurry," said Lev. He'd been in the cockpit and watched Astro long enough to know which lever was the throttle. He reached up to increase it when Astro placed a firm metal hand on his.

"We have to be careful, Leviathan," Astro advised. "Grogan topped off her boiler before we left but she's not used to all this travel. She's just a baby and not designed for swimming."

Lev thought about how afraid he had been to climb aboard when they escaped from the rampart of the castle. So much had happened in such a short time. "What's her name?" Lev asked.

"What?" Astro said, pulling back levers as they dove into the depths off the ridge.

"Her name? Does this dragonfly bot have a name?"

Astro smiled. "No, I don't think so."

"She needs one. That way we can talk to her," Lev said aloud and the dragon fly squawked.

Astro was focused on following Maurea's instructions. Lev sat back and let his mind flip through possible names.

Astro gave him a side glance. "How about DF6511?"

"What about it?"

"As a name."

"That's not a name. She needs a name like Brody or Astro or Grunt," Lev explained.

"Those are just what we call each other, but when we were born, Grogan gave us official names."

"What's your official name?" Lev asked.

Astro puffed out his chest with pride. "I am A57R0."

Lev let the numbers and letters form a picture in his mind. It looked a lot like Astro.

"Why Astro?" Lev asked.

"It is my deep desire to someday go to the stars. I want to be an astronaut."

"Can we go to space with steam power?" Lev asked.

"Not yet. If anyone can figure out a way, it's Grogan," Astro said.

"So," Lev asked sheepishly, "robots have dreams?"

"Sure they do. Or at least those of us built by Grogan. We all have dreams. I want to be an astronaut. Grunt wants to have an animal rescue preserve and save kittens." Lev thought about the immense robot surrounding himself in tiny balls of fluff. He laughed.

"What does Brody dream of?" Lev asked.

Astro sighed. "I'm not sure. It has been a long time since he and I have spent any time together. He has been away all these years protecting you. His letters are filled with saying how much he enjoys his time with you. Maybe he has other dreams but if he does, he has not expressed them to me. He is happy spending his time with you. And that's what matters. Our dreams and our happiness as robots are what make us unique."

Lev thought about what made the dragonfly special. He was growing very fond of her since she had rescued him from Nautilus Castle. "What about Bat?"

"Bat?" Astro asked.

"Sure," said Lev. "She can navigate in the dark and do acrobatics. Plus she can fly and swim but I think bats are kinda cool. What do you think?"

"I like it." Astro agreed. He flipped a switch to the intercom. "Lev wants to name you Bat. How does that sound to you, girl?"

The dragonfly was busy using her wings like oars on a boat as she propelled them through the ocean. She gave a happy purr. Lev and Astro laughed.

"I think she likes it," Astro said, giving Lev a wink with one shutter of his optic sensor. "Ok, according to these directions, it's time for a deep dive. Bat, we're going to need some light if we're going to be able to see where we're going."

There was a small release of steam from outside of the cockpit. Mobile, metal panels slid out to each side of the transport's head revealing lights here Bat's eyes were stationed. The surrounding, dark water glowed in front of them. Lev shivered as they dove and he felt the temperature drop inside the cockpit.

Strange creatures swam past the windshield the closer they made their way to the ocean floor. There were fish that glowed by their own luminescence and some who were nearly invisible because their skins were translucent. Some had bulging eyes that made Lev wrinkle his nose and others looked like ghosts flying in a night sky.

"Ok," said Astro. "Now we level out and follow this course until we come to an old wreck called The Dream."

Before long, Bat, Astro and Lev could see movement up ahead of them. At first, Lev thought it was a strange shimmer of the water. But then he realized that the shimmer had eyes and teeth. Sea snakes. The serpents patrolled the ancient shipwreck that sat on an ocean floor in the dark waters of this cold and lonely depth. This was the lair of Madame Haaf.

Lev recognized the ship from one of the books he'd found in the Knight's donation box. While he wasn't allowed a tutor like Amelia, he had been given free reign to read or study any book left for the poor. He had loved one copy that was filled with stories and pictures of sailing ships and steamers. He could see that this boat had been a schooner. Wisps of cloth were the only remains of the glorious sails that had once clung to the two, immense masts. Below deck, a green light glowed and seeped above through the rotting floor boards. Astro and Lev stared through the cockpit windshield, summoning their courage.

An idea sparked in Lev's mind and he reached into the parcel from Maurea, pulling out the shells of soup. "I'll take these as a gift. I imagine you shouldn't go visit a sea witch without bringing her a present."

"Good idea, but what had Maurea said about the snakes? Don't we need to give them something?" Brody reminded Lev.

Lev's hand hovered over the release lever of the cockpit windshield and took a deep breath, "Right. Ok. I'll be right back."

"Oh no you don't," argued Astro, stopping Lev from swimming out of the cockpit. "I'm not letting you talk to an Enchantress or her sea snakes alone. Brody might be your best friend but he's my brother. We go together," Astro insisted.

The cockpit opened and Lev shivered as the cold water washed over him. His scales and royal coloring returned and Astro gave him a thumbs up under the glow and safety of Bat's lights. The dragonfly followed the two until she was stopped by two flanking snakes at the edge of a wooden plank attached to the ship.

"Ah, the half-mer prince is here," said one snake.

"Our lady has been waiting a long time, I fear" said the other.

"Leave your metal man here," said the first.

"No," Lev managed to say, swallowing back his revulsion at their milky, blind eyes and jagged, pointed teeth. "He's with me."

"Our lady does not like metal men, my dear," said the second.

"I don't like snakes and yet here we are talking to you," Astro retorted.

The pair of serpents hissed and barred their teeth but they let the two friends pass and walk up the gang plank and on to the schooner. Two more sea snakes shimmered as if from thin air and joined their siblings, staring at them hungrily.

"They smell delicious," remarked one as it swam in circles around Lev and Brody, making the two feel trapped in a ring of bubbles.

"That's not us, that's the gifts we brought for you and your lady. We will just go see her now," Astro hedged as he tried to make his way past the four guards. He was met with a sharp snap as the snake's jaws clamped shut, barely missing Astro's nose.

"We are guests!" Lev insisted.

"Don't be so vicious! We can't help when we smell delicious," argued one snake. "Do any of you remember sending out invitations?"

"No, but they came any ways. How gracious," sang the other three.

"Then, I say we have them AND whatever they've brought with them for our lunch," said number one.

"We love it when their bones go crunch!," sang the other three.

At the sound of the last word, all four snakes dove for the two friends. At nearly the same moment, the sound of an explosion sent Lev to his knees and Astro bending to shield Lev's body. Following the boom was a thundering voice that seemed to come out of the cloud of smoke on deck.

"ENOUGH!" Madame Haaf shouted. "How dare you worms attack anyone on MY ship without my say?!"

A barrel instantly appeared on deck and she propped her right shoe on it. "Maybe I skin the four of you alive and make myself a new pair of boots! Isn't that what they do on land? What say you royal half-mer?"

There was a pause and Astro nudged Lev who didn't realize in his shock of seeing the Enchantress that she was talking to him. "Oh, snake skins, boots yes, yes they make boots from snakes on shore."

"See what I been tellin' you?" Madame Haaf said as she waved her finger at the four cowering serpents. "If you ain't gonna listen, you know what's comin'!" At that, the four guardians of the schooner took off for fear of becoming her new pair of footwear.

Madame Haaf turned to Lev and Astro. "Good, they're gone. Now we can have a proper talk, I think. But where are my manners? Come inside."

With a wave of her scaly finger, a shining staircase appeared near their feet leading to the belly of the boat. "After you," she gestured.

Every instinct told Lev not to leave the topside of the deck. But what had Maurea said? Madame Haaf was his mother's friend. Surely he could trust her. Still he hesitated.

"Aww. Don't be afraid young half-mer. I see your mother in your eyes. No harm will come to you here."

Lev gave his best smile but it was a struggle. The enchantress had the face of a salt water crocodile and the body of a woman. Her gaze was fierce and Lev thought she wanted him for a snack more than she wanted be his friend. Sensing the tension, Astro put himself between her and Lev as the friends made their way down the stairs.

Inside the main cabin was an old fashioned living room complete with velvet chairs and green glowing reading lamps. Lev was sure it was some kind of spell. She waved her hand to sit and two of the chairs skated across the floor, scooping up Lev and Astro. Lev stood to reach for his bag and blanched. Madame Haaf was already looking through it without an invitation. "Oh," he said, "I brought those for you. Homemade soup."

"You cooked a potion for me? When does the royal boy have time to make an old witch a brew?" Madame Haaf mused.

"Oh, uh no. My friend made it. It's really good. I thought you might like some too."

She took the shells of soup and smiled but her yellow, serpentine eyes still glared at him. "So much like your mother," she said. Then she looked at Astro. "And you, man made of metal, what have you brought for me?"

Astro sat upright in his chair and squirmed uncomfortably. His expression looked panicked. Lev spoke up and gave a nervous chuckle. "He brought me! I mean, I'm his gift."

A wicked smirk spread across her terrible mouth. "So I can keep you for myself?" Madame asked.

Now it was Lev's turn to panic. "Oh, no. I mean, he brought me here...err...to visit. We heard that maybe you wanted to visit with me?" It was more of a question than a statement. "You know, because someone said you knew my mother?"

"A visit is all you came for? Hmm? I don't serve tea and cookies, Prince. Be honest. That is the first sign of a good ruler. Don't you want something else from me too?" Madame asked running her clawed fingers over the edge of the sofa, staring at Lev as if he was a snack.

Lev could feel his legs begin to tremble but he laughed to cover it up.

"Relax child," she said finally. "I know why you're here and none too soon. King Milos has heard all the commotion going on in the waters above his kingdom. You sure do make a lot of racket for one small boy. He is not happy about the pirates and metal men so close to his realm. And he is not happy that his half-mer son has not arrived to pledge his loyalty to his father and the underwater crown."

"King Milos knows I'm here?" Lev gulped.

"Oh yes, boy. He knows and he's as angry a nest of hornets. He is looking for you while the battle rages topside," said the witch.

"Battle?!" Astro was on his feet.

"Yes. Seems all you men do is fight. No matter if you're made of skin and bone or steal and iron. Grogan was unable to negotiate for Brody's life and now the metal army fights against the living and dead of Green Beard's crew. Take a look for yourself."

Madame Haaf tapped her left eye and it popped into the palm of her hand. Lev gripped him stomach as it lurched at the sight. His reaction made her laugh an awful, wicked laugh. She insisted

Lev take her eye in his own hand anyways and look through the back of it. "See through my eyes, Prince," she said.

Lev stared at it unsure but Astro was too compelled by the words of battle to be squeamish. The robot took Madame Haas's eye and held it up to his optic shutter. It was as if they were looking through a telescope. Pirates and robots were in close combat, blade to blade. Razor was sword to sword with Slice. Dozens of spider bots were crawling all over Green Beard's deck. There was no sign of Brody or Grogan. Astro lowered the eye and held it in front of Lev's face so he could see too.

The spiders had little effect on the pirates, save the few who were afraid of spiders. Their venom was useless. Lev wondered why it didn't work on the pirates who were alive. Grunt was dueling with a skeleton wearing an eye patch. The huge robot hit the pirate with one blow of his immense fist. The skeleton's bones flew apart but within seconds reassembled themselves. Lev felt his insides twist. His friends were losing.

The eye sprang up and flew across the cabin. It popped into the empty socked of Madame Haaf's face. "Now you two look sorrier than a kitten at a dog show."

"A what?" Astro asked.

"Never you mind. Hush up and listen. You know what my daddy used to do when times got hard? He would tell me a story. Now, I'm gonna tell you one."

The crocodile witch glided across the cabin of her underwater schooner, her robes of midnight blue flecked with stars swayed in the water currents.

"Once upon a time, (like every good story should start), there was a young man. He was handsome and strong and had big plans for his big life. He had a cart in the village where he sold tools for building things and lava rocks for cooking. One day, an old farmer came to his cart to buy a knife for cutting back kelp in his patch of the forest. When the young man told the old man the price, the old man took out an old scroll of leather from his pocket instead of coins.

At first the young man yelled and told the old man to go away. But the old man persisted and unrolled the scroll, revealing a map. Now he had the young man's attention. The old man said that he had once been a pirate and had won the map in a game of Davey Jones Locker. He had always planned to follow the map and find the treasure once he had enough men to sail to the topside. Alas, the years passed and the old pirate never could gather a crew and ship. The young man stared at the map, unable to believe his good fortune.

And so the younger man agreed to the trade, he looked up to give the old pirate his knife but the old man had vanished. For weeks after that, the young man tried to convince the men of the town to join him on an adventure. The men just laughed at him. Every night, he counted his money. He did not have enough to buy a proper ship.

Then, one evening, while he was having his supper in the local tavern, he watched as the king's soldiers entered. They walked through the tavern and took the men who were asleep at their tables or had been fighting when the soldiers had walked in.

The young man followed behind silently as he watched the king's soldiers lock the men in irons and force them on to the royal naval ships. That gave him an idea.

The next morning, he dressed in his finest clothes and went to the castle. He stood in the hallways and pretended to be a footman. He watched as the cook took a tray in to the royal suite at breakfast. The young man hid in the hallway until lunchtime. Just before the cook made it to the suite once again with the midday meal, the young man whispered to the cook from around the corner. Taking some of his coins from his pocket, he paid the cook to change places with him for ten minutes. The cook was not paid much by the crown and agreed but only for a few minutes.

The young man put on the cook's jacket and hat and pushed the cart with the king's lunch into the royal suite. There, he found the king resting in his bed. No one knows what happened in those next, few short minutes. The young man had gone in with the idea that he would show the king the map and ask for soldiers and men to have an adventure and dig for treasure. He would share the gold with the king.

Did the king refuse? Did he laugh at the young man? Remember, he wanted a big life. No one knows how it happened. All we do know is that by the next morning, the old king was dead and the young man, King Milos was crowned the new king.

"What?" Lev gasped.

Madame Haaf continued. "The next morning, he gathered all of the kingdoms='s subjects into the square to issue a new set of rules. The people were suspicious of the new king. They did not want to follow new rules or pay higher taxes. They did not love him. Many men stood up and demanded to know what happened to the old king. Those men were immediately arrested and locked in the dungeon.

He never earned the people's trust. Instead, he ruled with a fist of iron. (No offense metal man.)"

"None taken," Astro said.

"And so, King Milos became known as Milos the Murderer to the people. He made them pay heavy taxes. He put the poor and the orphans in jail. Any prisoner who spoke ill of the king was executed.

One day, he sent his soldiers out to find him a bride to be his queen. Every woman refused. The King had made the big life he had planned as well as a kingdom but he needed a queen to have heirs.

That's when King Milos wrote to your grandfather and struck a bargain for Queen Anna's hand in marriage. King Milos promised that if Queen Anna agreed to marry him, then his army would never attack Nautilus Castle or its people. But, if she refused, he would consider it an act of war.

"My poor mother," Lev whispered.

"Indeed," agreed Madame Haaf.

"Whatever happened to the treasure map?" Lev asked.

"I'm so glad that you have asked this question. You are a clever boy," said the Enchantress.

"Your mother hated her life after marrying King Milos. She sent a desperate message to Grogan. Many rumors spread that she was wrong to see her old love, Grogan. But she was not seeing him out of love. She snuck Grogan in to the castle asking him to help her make a plan to escape with you.

When she found out that she was going to have a baby, she knew she could not trust King Milos to be kind to you. His cruelty with his people was growing stronger. In her daily walks and wanderings of the lonely castle, she stumbled into a small room she'd never seen before. She thought, perhaps it might be a place where she could hide with you if the King's temper threatened your safety.

Every night, your mother went to the room and hid things in it that she thought you might need in an emergency. One night, she pulled some books off of a shelf and from between the books something fell to the floor."

"The map," Astro said.

"Yes. The old pirate's mysterious map was there in Anna's hands. Milos no longer needed it. He had all the gold and power he could want. Instead, he had hidden it away in a room far from the throne and forgotten about it."

One night, while making plans for her escape, Grogan and Anna were discovered by the king's men. Her plan had been to take Grogan to the room so he could find her if the two of you were hiding. She also wanted to show him the map she had found."

Lev interrupted, "But Green Beard and Razor followed them and set off the alarm by stealing some of the king's gold."

"Yes, so you do know part of the story."

"What ever happened to the map?" Lev asked again.

"King Milos locked your mother in that very room, making wait to give birth to you. His guards said that he wanted to lock her in the dungeon but the soldiers refused."

"Did he put Grogan in the dungeon?" Lev asked.

"Yes. Grogan was scheduled to be executed the next morning. That night, the army of tiny spiders infiltrated the dungeon and freed Grogan. He tried to rescue Anna too but there were too many guards."

"When the time came for you to be born, Queen Anna called for me, the royal healer working in the kingdom at the time to come to help her."

"You were there when I was born?" Lev asked incredulously.

"I was. You see, your mother was put under one of my enchantments so that she could breathe under water in her new home. She was afraid that you might drown if you were not born with gills."

Lev unconsciously touched the gills on the sides of his neck.

" After she gave birth to you, and the two of you were resting, she handed me a small basket as a thank you. No one thought anything of this. Your mother was always very kind and generous.

When I returned home, I opened the basket to find the map and a note explaining that I should keep it hidden and safe until her son could return to the sea and claim the treasure for himself. With the treasure, her son, a good Prince could defeat King Milos and restore peace in the kingdom."

Lev stared at Madame Haaf in disbelief. "I'm just a kid. I can't defeat a king."

"And yet, here you are at the bottom of the ocean talking to the witch of the sea," she laughed.

"I can't save a kingdom," he argued.

A map shimmered into view in the Enchantress's hand. Astro stood and stared at it, his optic sensors as wide as saucers. Astro suggested, "But you could trade a map to a pirate in exchange for a prisoner or two…"

"Ha!," cackled Madame Haaf. She clutched the map and held it tight to her chest. "You think you can make a deal with the devil and expect him to be honest about his end of the bargain?," she yelled. "No! Green Beard will happily take the map but he will never set your family free if he thinks he can control a young prince."

"But we need to save Brody. He's my… he's all I have left.." Lev argued, exhausted. He was hungry again. He was cold and his heart ached for the only family he'd ever known.

"What will you do if your Brody is free?" Madame asked as she stared at him hard.

Lev didn't answer. What would he do? He thought of his mother and all the people who loved her like Ezra and Maurea. He looked at the map in the witch's fingers. He rubbed the medallion around his neck. Finally, he looked up at Madame Haaf.

"Why aren't you in the kingdom anymore?" Lev asked.

The Enchantress gave him a side glance as she squinted in suspicion at his question. "King Milos banished me after you and you mother disappeared. He accused me of helping her."

"Did you help her?" Astro asked.

"Sometimes we have to be brave and willing to lose what we have gained in order for justice to live. I was a healer, a doctor, as you say. She came to see me the night she fled to Nautilus Castle with you." Madame Haaf sighed. "We knew you were born with gills. You could breathe under the water. We did not know if you could breathe above the water. So, I enchanted the metal man."

"What do you mean?" Astro asked. "They found Brody in pieces that night on the shore."

"Yes. It was a risk and Brody agreed to take it in the event that you could not breathe above the water."

"Wait, I don't understand," Lev argued.

"Enough!" The enchantress bellowed and he held the map high in the glow of the green lights with her midnight cape and glowing stars below it. "Enough of this for now! Answer the question boy, what will you do if your friends are free? What will you do if the map declares you worthy?"

<u>Thirteen</u>

A treasure map. Is there anything better than having an adventure at sea with your friends? Lev had read books about boats and high seas, pirates and treasure. Still, this wasn't a storybook was it? When he read the book, his heart pumped wildly at the description of sword fights and walking the plank. When it happened for real, any number of terrible things really could happen to his friends.

Yet, he was a prince now and Brody had protected him his whole life. Brody was a prisoner of Green Beard because he had been trying to save Lev. He owed it to Brody. If Grogan was captured, he owed him a rescue too. Hadn't Grogan kept the queen from sending him away? If it weren't for Grogan, he wouldn't even know he was a prince, or how him mother loved him and wanted to protect him.

Lev thought all of this as he stared up in to the collection of labeled bottles that lined the shelves of Madame Haaf's salon. His gaze returned to the map. Something pricked in the back of his mind. He turned to the witch. "Why don't you follow the map?"

The crocodile witch scowled. "I told you, half-boy. I promised your mother. A promise is a sacred thing, even for someone like me."

An anger like he'd never felt before surged through his whole body. Lev thought of his poor mother and all she had suffered. He thought of the lonely years he spent hidden away in the tower at Nautilus Castle. It was like he and his mother could hear and feel things others couldn't but no one would listen to either of them. "My mother is dead! And maybe my best friend too who apparently did more than just travel to protect me, so answer the question!" Lev shouted. His fists were in tight balls and he began to sift water through his gills so hard he could feel a current swirling around him. "With all of your power and spells and enchantments, why don't you go get the stupid treasure yourself?!"

Madame watched him warily. She gritted her teeth and said, "I haven't gone after the treasure because the map won't reveal itself to me! It will only show the way to someone who is destined to rule." He and the witch were snout to nose and Lev didn't care.

"So now we have the truth," Astro spat. "It was never about a gift for Lev from his mother. You need him to read the map."

Madame Haaf shrugged. "So what if I do? So what?"

"What do you want if Lev goes to get the treasure?" Astro sighed.

"I already gave him the biggest gift. I gave him knowledge of his mother. I gave him his birth story and most of all, I gave him a warning of the cruelty of King Milos," Madame Haaf argued.

"Right, and you want me to read the map for you in return. I can't imagine you actually like living in exile here in the bottom of the sea," Lev said. "You need the treasure to leave here."

Madame Haaf shed a crocodile tear and batted her eyes. This time, Lev saw all of her rows of her crooked teeth. It made him want to swim away as fast as he could. In the same breath, he wished he could just banish her himself. All of this had been a trick. She confessed, "I want to be restored to royal healer when you become king. I want to take care of patients again. And, of course, a royal salary with rooms in the palace. Hmm?"

"Money and power, of course," Astro said, anger in his voice.

Lev folded his arms. "So you don't want to go and buy an island or something. You want to go after the treasure and give it to me?" Lev was suspicious.

"I want you to be the new King and that will take all the gold we can get our hands on," replied the Enchantress.

Lev felt his heart in his throat. He held out his hand as he listened to the high pitched ringing in his ears whenever something big was happening in his small life. "If you get Brody and Grogan out of Green Beard's prison alive, I will take the map and go after the treasure."

The Enchantress pulled the map even closer to her body. "And restore the kingdom, taking your seat as king?"

"Sure. If I live that long," Lev said. He doubted any of them would make it that far but what did he have to lose? At least Brody and Grogan would be free. If things really went well, he'd be king. A little piece of him laughed at that. He could just imagine the look on Princess Amelia's face. He held out his hand. "Only one way to find out if we have a deal. Let's see if the map shows itself to me. Let's see if I'm meant to rule." Secretly, he wondered how a map could know his destiny.

Slowly, Madame Haaf handed him the map. With a snap of her fingers, a table appeared beside

Lev. He untied the leather band that held it together and the scroll opened without assistance. Words, as if they were floating up to the surface of the ocean appeared in wavy, watery letters. Lev read aloud,

"Fish and bone and beds of kelp,
The Milos kingdom cries for help.
Follow me and test your measure,
Friendship is the greatest treasure."

Madame Haaf smiled. "I do believe have a bargain, your majesty."

"Help me save my friends and yes, we have a bargain," Lev agreed.

The witch moved like lightning, a trail of bubbles behind her as she propelled her body through the cabin of the ship, collecting things and placing them in a bag. She closed one eye but kept the one Lev had held in his hand open.

"We must be quick about it," she shouted. "Call to battle!" Madame shouted out into the water. Her four sea snakes appeared from the shadowy hiding places on the ship.

The four bowed their heads and slithered around Madame's neck. "Head to the surface or you will be boots by morning. You feast on pirates tonight," she directed. Lev looked at Madame Haaf's clawed feet. He wondered if she really needed boots at all.

"Prince and Metal Man," she ordered. "Go back to your farmers and bring as many of them as you can."

"What are we going to do, bribe them with sea cucumbers?" Astro said, sarcastically.

"Look at you, all metal and shiny and thinking you know everything. Do you know why Green Beard has never been defeated?" Madame asked, ignoring Astro's sarcasm. She didn't wait for a reply. "He's only half alive! The other half is skeleton; undead. Part of him fell into the Black Sea a long time ago. (That's another story.) Now, do you know how you defeat the undead?" The two friends shook their heads.

"You say their name," she replied.

"Green Beard?" Lev asked.

"No mother ever gave a child the name Green Beard! You got to say his real name, the one his mama gave him."

"How do we find that out?" Astro asked.

"You got your job and I got mine." She patted the bag full of potions and trinkets as the side of her mouth twisted into a sly grin. "Now go! Meet me topside. Bring your loyal subjects, young prince." She glared at him. "And don't you lose that map." Then, she laughed.

Madame Haaf and her sea snakes disappeared with a swish of her midnight robe. Her wicked laugh, on the other hand, stayed behind. Lev's eyes darted around the room. He shuddered. Lev heard Astro's optic sensors widen and narrow.

Astro and Lev looked to one another. "Do you think she's gone?" Astro whispered.

"I hope so," confessed Lev. "That woman is scary."

As the enchantress's laugh faded, an ornate potions bottle shimmered into being on the table next to Lev. "Now what?" Astro wondered aloud.

Lev read the label on the bottle, "Big-eyed Scad." Lev turned to Astro, "That sounds terrible."

Astro laughed, "It's a fish that can turn itself invisible."

Lev swished the bottle round and peered inside as he held it up to the glowing lamp light. "I don't see a fish in there."

Astro teased, "Maybe that's the point."

Lev rolled his eyes. "We'll take it with is just in case."

Astro nodded. He took Lev's hand, "Congratulations, you're a confirmed prince now. You also have a treasure map that speaks directly to you. Wait til Brody hears this!" Astro smiled. "Things are looking up!"

Lev let out a weak laugh. "Yeah. I know, it's great." He didn't have the heart to tell Astro that the idea of the whole thing felt impossible. He kind of wished that instead of a prince, he was a Big-eyed Scad and could become invisible for a little while.

<u>Fourteen</u>

"Come on girl, you can do it!" Lev said as he patted the cockpit of Bat, the transport bot. She was tired and her steam engine was having trouble firing up in the cold water of the deep. Astro and Lev were in a hurry to return to Ezra and Maurea and the rest of their village. Finally, with a little coaxing, she found her spark and the engine came to life. Bat swam as fast as she could but she was running out of steam in her engine.

"We can't exhaust her," Astro counseled. "We'll need to make it up the surface near the Kismet once we gather the villagers together."

While luck seemed to be with them in the schooner, the trip back to the village seemed like it was taking forever. Lev sat back and imagined a plan in his head. He listed his assets like Grunt, Slice, Astro and hopefully Brody and few other technical robots who were still on the Kismet. There were the venomous spiders. Then, he considered the farmers and fishers from Ezra's village. How could so few defeat Green Beard? Ideas and an offense started to form. He'd need to get Grogan and Brody off of the Graveyard first. Madame Haaf might be able to help with that.

It took hours but Lev used the time to make battle plans and reduce attempts in his head. "Almost there," Astro said, breaking Lev's concentration.

Bat suddenly seized controls from Astro and stopped dead in the water. She chirped and squawked transmitting her warning to the cockpit.

"What's she saying?" Lev asked. "What's wrong, girl? Do you need a rest?"

Astro turned a dial and Bat's message was translated to broadcast over the internal cockpit speaker. "Mollusk Men. Mollusk Men ahead! Must hide."

Astro tried to take the controls, but Bat turned herself east and hid them behind the ridge. Lev and Astro argued with her, but she wouldn't listen.

"What are Mollusk Men? We don't have time for this. We've got to get to Ezra and the others."

Astro's optic shutters whirled frantically as he zeroed in on the direction of the village. "Bat may have just saved us. Mollusk Men are what the people outside of the kingdom wall call King Milos's soldiers. They are brutal. They attach mollusk shells to the bottom of their transports so that whatever they glide over is shredded; villagers, seaweed, coral reefs, whatever, they don't care who or what they destroy in their path.

Lev closed his eyes and listened. He was sure he heard cries for help. "We can't just leave them, Astro. King Milos sent his soldiers to find me, not them."

"But the generals of that army will use Ezra and the villagers as bait to lure you in, hoping that you try to save them. If we go down there, we're playing right into their hands."

"And if we don't help them, they will suffer because they helped me," Lev argued. He was very quiet for a minute as a thought burst into brilliance in his brain. He gave a laugh and took out the bottle from Madame Haaf. "You're right Astro. As the prince, I would be caught the second the soldiers saw me."

"Good, I'm glad you're coming to your senses," Astro agreed.

"But what if the soldiers never saw me?" Lev asked as he held up the bottle of potion.

"No," Astro objected, "we have no idea what that stuff could really do."

"How does a scad go invisible?"

"It's body reflects light in such a way that you can't see it," Brody explained.

Lev popped the cork from the potion. "Sounds perfect." Before Astro could stop him, Lev gulped down the contents of the bottle. He winced at the flavor. "Awful," he managed.

Astro stared at him. "Any idea how long it lasts?"

"Nope," Lev confessed. "How long until it takes effect?"

"I'd say right away. You shimmered out of sight them minute you started drinking it."

"Wow," Lev said with some excitement he couldn't hide. "I'll go get Ezra, Maurea and as many villagers as I can. See you soon."

The cockpit opened once again and Lev swam out as fast as he could directly towards the village. Once at the ridge, he followed it down to the kelp wall the hid the entrance to Ezra's house. Soldiers were shouting just a few yards away but he managed to slip through the ribbons and go inside.

Maurea, Ezra and several children were hiding near the corner of the stove. "Ezra," Lev whispered. The mermaid looked around the room. "Ezra it's me, Leviathan."

"Where are you?" Ezra asked.

"I'm here. You just can't see me in the light. Hang on." Lev joined them, huddled in the dark and without the light of the room, he came into view. Before he understood what was happening, Ezra threw her arms around him and wrapped him in a hug.

"I'm so glad you are safe," she whispered.

His heart beat quickened as he hugged her back. Then he looked at her and the rest. "Astro and Bat are just up the ridge. I will take you one by one."

"But we aren't invisible like you," Ezra pointed out.

Maurea shook her head. "There isn't enough room for all of us in your robot machine, anyways. You will need one of our boats to carry us all."

Lev realized he hadn't thought it through. Where did he think they'd all go? He had been too excited with the thought of being invisible. Why didn't the sea witch give him a giant swimming carpet or a magical submarine while she was at it?

Maurea continued, "We could take my boat but Captain Calico has taken my keys. She and Lev tiptoed to the kelp ribbon door and pulled one strip aside to sneak a peek.

"Which one is he?" Lev asked as they looked out on to the village and soldiers.

"She is over there. That's Captain Calico. She's head of the Mollusk Men," said Maurea, pointing to a large squid dressed in a royal uniform of the Meridium Kingdom.

Lev gulped. The squid captain was shouting orders to one of her soldiers while she held one villager in one tentacle and his information papers in another. She held both up as her other six legs propelled her to a tall cage where the other villagers had been detained.

"I don't see any authorization here from the king giving you permission to leave the castle walls, therefore, you are an enemy of the crown and will be thrown in the dungeon. Her one arm threw his papers into a trash can while another opened the lock of the cage. She threw the mer-man in and locked the gate once more.

"Is that everyone? I was told the long lost prince would be here!" Calico sounded annoyed.

The villagers stayed silent.

"And where are all of the children? Don't you peasants usually have children running around?"

Again, the parents said nothing.

"Fine," smirked the squid. "Sergeant, send in the Mixer!"

Several soldiers pushed a machine forward towards the center of the village. Lev watched as the men turned it slowly into position.

"What's the mixer?" Lev asked as he heard Maurea gasp.

Maurea's voice began to crack. "It creates a giant wave under the sea. Everything in the wave is washed away. The Mollusk Men have wiped out entire villages and everyone in them with just one wave."

Before she could say anymore, Lev slipped out the door undetected and swam straight for Captain Calico. He counted carefully to himself, "One, two, three, four, five, six, seven." Maurea gasped because she was sure that Lev, in all of his swimming was sure to collide face to face with the squid. At the last minute, the boy pulled himself up as quick as he could and then dove hard, landing himself right behind the Captain. As he suspected, she was holding the keys to the boat in her eighth tentacle, hidden behind her back.

'Okay', he thought to himself. 'I've found the keys. Now how to get them away from her and fast.' He looked for a distraction. A stack of tools near a farm shed was the perfect solution.

Lev threw a huge pair of scissor-like things, up just over the Captain's head. They floated up and then sank, knocking her in the head. "What the?" Lev heard her say as she picked the up to examine them. She turned around but saw nothing.

Encouraged by her reaction, Lev threw a shovel, a hoe, a rake, a yolk for a sea cow and a crate half full of sea cucumbers that floated up and then rained down like delicate snowflakes of confusion. In her attempt to catch the larger items, Captain Calico dropped the keys. They slowly floated to the sandy floor. Lev carefully picked them up. He slowly and delicately swam out from behind the squid, careful not to stir the sand. Once cleared, he began swimming as fast as he could.

The squid was confused and started shouting and barking orders to equally confused soldiers. A bit of chaos was a good thing, Lev decided to use the opportunity swim over and hide inside of Maurea's boat. Once inside, crouched down, his heart jumped up into his throat. He realized he'd never driven an underwater transport of any kind. 'Who am I kidding?' he thought. 'I've never driven anything in my whole life!' Why had he told Astro to stay hidden?'

Lev figured where the old fashioned ignition was, held his breath and inserted the key. Before he could second guess himself, he started the steam engine. The boat roared to life and all of the cover of chaos stopped to stare at the boat with the no driver. Every Mollusk Man as well their captain stared at the boat that began moving through the square as if under its own power.

Lev found the throttle and nearly fell backwards and out of the boat from the force. He headed straight for Maurea's house. Somewhere between the square and the hidden door, he found the break and pulled the lever with all of his strength before he hit Ezra and her house.

"Get it!" Lev shouted.

The sound of scrambling came from within the house as well as behind him. Ezra carried two smaller children in her arms while Maurea held the hands of two older kids. One by one they leaped into the boat, wherever they could find room.

Meanwhile, the Mollusk Men had assembled with militant precision. They aimed the Mixer directly at Lev and his passengers. Lev pushed the throttle once again but had trouble keeping control. They were spinning in circles, the kids were screaming and laughing, Maurea gripped her seat and Ezra was pointing at the Mixer that was getting closer and closer. Captain Calico was powering it up.

Astro jumped in the boat and made everyone but Lev scream. "Where have you been?" Lev asked.

"Trying to catch up to you! You're not so easy to find when you're invisible, you know. Here," he handed Lev his skateboard. "Jump on this and head towards Bat. I'll drive the boat. When that Mixer goes off, we don't want to be anywhere near it."

Under Astro's expert skill, the boat took off towards the ridge where Bat was waiting. She chirped and clicked as she opened her cockpit just waiting to take on passengers. "Not now, Astro told her through com link. We need to get out of here fast. Pick Lev up. He's on his way to you. Head for open water. It's our safest bet.

Lev thought of nothing else but the safety inside Bat's cockpit as he willed his board to glide through the water. He leaned forward and tucked his arms back as if he were flying, hoping to make himself propel through the water faster.

Then, they all heard The Mixer explode with it's powerful blades. An underwater tsunami poured from the deadly machine. "Climb! Climb! Swim high!" Astro shouted as he drove the boat up at nearly a ninety degree angle. The boat spun as it caught the edge of the wave but Astro fought the current. First maneuvering the boat into the crest of the wave and then rocketing the small boat out of the current.

When Bat had heard the machine, she dove behind the ridge, taking cover. Shards of coral and rock tumbled on to her head and wings. She cried out but Astro was too busy jettisoning up to the surface to help her.

Lev made it to her and, still riding his board, picked the rubble off of her. "It's ok girl, you're fine. Just a few dents but it's nothing to worry about."

Bat purred in relief. Just as Lev pushed his board out to make it around the to the other side of her, the edge of the board caught the Mixer's wave. Before he could understand what was happening, Lev was spinning and tumbling in the water.

When Astro and the others in the boat were safely far above the deep water wave, Captain Calico and the Mollusk Men, Ezra stood up and looked for Lev. He nor Bat were anywhere to be found. Astro widened his optic sensors as large as they would go but he didn't see his friend.

Desperately, Ezra began to call out for Lev. She started to sing….

Fifteen

Pain shot through Lev's skull. He'd been hit hard in the head by something. A strange thought ran through his mind as he and his steam powered surfboard collided with the giant wave created by The Mixer. He was spinning through the water, unable to know which way was up and which was down. 'I'm just like that girl, Alice,' he thought. 'Didn't she tumble to…where,' he stopped to think of the name of the land he had read about, 'oh yeah. Wonderland?'

He should have been afraid of where the wave might take him, far from his friends. He should have tried to see whether the Mollusk Men were in his wake. Instead, he was thinking about a story he had read on cold nights last winter. Every night, he had read a bit under the covers until he fell asleep. A pang of regret fluttered in his chest. 'I should have thanked the guards. Someone left that book for me in the clothing ration.'

He couldn't be sure he would ever see Nautilus Castle again or its knights. In his tumbling through the water he laughed morbidly. Lev wasn't sure he would survive the next fifteen minutes. Head over feet sinking and falling through the water with the board still tethered to his ankle by a cord. He couldn't swim out of the wave.

What had the White Rabbit said? He was late for a date. In his pounding headache, Lev too remembered he was late for something. He had to see someone or meet a person. He wished in that moment that he had a watch like the rabbit.

Leviathan Jones and the Sea Witch

Who did he have to meet? Lev fought hard to think in the violent, swirling world of water, sand, light and darkness. A wicked smile with pearly, sharp teeth appeared in his tumbling vision. One minute it looked like the cat in the story, the next, it changed into the awful, toothy smile of a half witch half crocodile. The face disappeared. A wicked Queen with red eyes and red lips replaced the cat and the croc. It wasn't Queen Eliza. Then he remembered. It was the Queen of Hearts. She was yelling something in a garden. A single playing card stared up at her, high on her throne. The Queen's face changed again. Instead of the Queen of Hearts, the vision became King Milos. He was sending them all to the dungeon. He had to get out of the dungeon. Lev rolled head over feet, over and over again. How could he escape the wave that stretched a as far as he could see?

He had to think. He wasn't in Wonderland. He was…in the ocean. That's right. He wasn't in a dungeon. He was trapped in a huge wave that was traveling under the surface of the sea. Finally a clear thought formed in his mind. He had a surfboard, why didn't he just ride the wave? It was too big and he was too small. Something told him to try anyways.

With every ounce of strength he had, Lev fought against the current and pushed his hand through the water, reaching his ankle. The tips of his fingers searched for the cord. The muscles in his arms ached but once he found the tether, he pulled it towards him. Reaching with his other hand, he gripped the cord and pulled again. Hand over hand, tumble. Tumble, pull and hold, pull and hold, tumble. It would take forever to get the board close enough but still he worked at it. 'Just stick with it,' he told himself.

Eventually, his hands felt the familiar shape of smooth wood. He knew there was no way he could stand on the board without the wave knocking him off again. Instead, Lev pulled the board to his chest, hugging it, maneuvering it to the wave crest. He had no idea which way was up or down but he locked his feet into the straps anyways and thought of the one person he longed to see in all the world.

"Brody," he told the surfboard. "Take me to Brody."

Grogan's magnificent invention bucked under Lev's body, and it took all of his strength to hold on. "Whoooaaaa!" Lev shouted as the board took off like a rocket, slicing though the wave. He and the surfboard spiraled like a corkscrew to escape the final pull of the wave. His fingers screamed under the pressure. Lev breathed a sigh of relief when he was free.

The board did not slow down. Instead, it aimed for the surface of the water like a torpedo. 'I'm on my way, Brody. Hang on,' Lev thought to himself. He wasn't sure how far The Mixer had taken him off course. He didn't recognize anything and he was clearly in the open ocean without reefs or ledges to give him a point of reference. His board seemed to know where it was going and so Lev hung on and put his head down, making himself streamline as he traveled through the water. He spent the time forming a plan for Brody's rescue in his mind and hoping that Madame Haaf had kept her end of the bargain.

On the edge of the water's surface, Ezra sang for a long time but there was no response. The silence of the azure blue sea made her stomach tight. Finally, it was Astro who made the decision. "Brody can't wait any longer. Leviathan will join us when he can," he added. Secretly, he hoped with all his might that it was very soon and that nothing happened to the boy.

The rescued villagers and their children joined Maurea as they tried to reassure Ezra. One small girl lifted her chin and held up a tiny shovel, "I'm going with you to fight the pirates!" Ezra put on her bravest smile but her heart ached for Leviathan and she couldn't explain why.

"All right, everyone. Climb in to your boats and let's head for the surface. I don't dare stay here too much longer for fear the Mollusk Men and Captain Calico might find us."

Maurea hugged her daughter. "I'm sure the prince will find his way back. Now go with Astro. You will be safe with him and Bat. I will bring the others."

Ezra agreed.

Quietly, the unlikely heroes floated up towards the surface following the homing beacon inside the Kismet. With luck, the Graveyard wouldn't be far away from it when they arrived.

As they made their way up, the water became lighter. Soon, several pods of dolphins joined their ascent. Elias and his pod gave Astro a click and a nod. Leviathan's little army was growing. Astro hoped that the boy was alive and on his way to rally his troops. He couldn't be sure that Madame Haaf would fulfill the contract of rescuing Brody without Lev.

The band of friends quietly surfaced near the Kismet. As Astro predicted, the Graveyard was only a few yards away, bobbing and swaying on the water as fighting between the two crews of the opposing ships continued. Astro's optic sensors scanned the deck of the pirate ship. There was no sign of Brody or Grogan.

Maurea and Ezra peered over the surface of the water in time to watch Grunt knock a living pirate into the water. The man screamed as his body and sword made a loud splash. The water that surrounded the man bubbled and foamed. His hand reached for the air, grasping for anything that might pull him out. Ezra's chest heaved and Maurea pulled her daughter close. The water exploded as if the ocean itself spat the pirate out.

This time, the pirate was completely changed. He had once been made of cloth and skin and eyes and muscles. The ocean returned the pirate to his deck with only threads a shirt, pants and boots. He was made of nothing but bones and teeth. For a moment, it was as if he turned and glared directly at the mother and daughter with his hollow eye sockets. The two dove deep in the hopes that they imagined it, clinging to one another.

When Ezra opened her eyes, she did scream. Something was coming at them from the deep waters and fast. Neither of them knew which way to go. To surface meant to fight against the pirates who couldn't seem to be killed. Below, something neither could make out that would soon be upon them. Ezra screamed for the only thing she could think of that was larger and hopefully stronger than the enemy from the depths. "Bat!!" Ezra called out.

The dragonfly transport had powered down after it's exhausting swim. At the sound of her name, though, Bat's eyes became beacons and she fluttered her wings. Her sensors detected and recognized the voice calling her as Ezra. Bat's radar searched the ocean for the source that was the mermaid. As Bat honed in on Ezra's call, she started her engine with only a quarter tank of fresh water and fired up her internal boiler, steaming her way as fast as she could towards the call of distress.

Maurea wrapped her tail protectively around Ezra. The dark water concealed the exact shape of whatever was approaching. She could tell that the something had two parts. It's bottom was darker and larger than it's top. Bat clicked and chirped to the two of them. She wasn't far, but encouraged Maurea and Ezra to swim towards her. Bat opened her cockpit belly as she sped to the aid of her friends.

"Swim!" Maurea shouted as she and Ezra propelled themselves through the water as fast as they could to meet Bat. Bubbles from the deep encouraged them to swim faster, arching their tails up and down while their hands cut through the water.

The two tumbled inside, pulling in their tails as Bat quickly closed the cockpit door protectively. Ezra looked out the class windshield to watch whatever it was pass them in a thick cloud of bubbles, seaweed and color. "What is it?!" Maurea asked, staring out the glass.

Ezra sharpened her gaze and squealed. There was a glimmer of hope in her as she pressed herself closer to the glass. "I don't think that's a sea monster after all."

"Don't be ridiculous, child. What else could it be?" Maurea argued.

Bat began to bounce up and down, chirping and clicking happily. Her sensors had picked up and confirmed the approaching object. Leviathan circled back to Bat and as he surfed to his transport bot he slowed down. There was Ezra waving frantically in the window of the cockpit at him. He waved back. Ezra squirmed out of the cockpit as soon as it began to reopen and she swam to Lev. She hugged him so hard the two nearly fell off of his board.

"We thought you were...we thought that Captain Calico..."she stammered.

"I know," Lev shrugged. "But I'm here now."

"The pirates," Ezra continued, "if they fall in the water," she shuddered.

"Skeletons?" Lev asked.

Ezra nodded.

"So Madame Haaf was right."

"How can we possibly win against an enemy who cannot die?" Ezra asked desperately.

"Oh they can die. It's just a little bit tricky," Lev said.

The water began to shimmer and swirl all around them. Lev pulled Ezra completely on to his board in case they needed a quick escape. He'd seen water do that once before and he didn't like it happening so close to him or Ezra.

"We see the boy is more than a prince," said one snake as it came into view.

"He must fight before his kiss," said another.

"Our mistress goes to set the net," sang the third snake.

"Then you send them to the icy depths," cooed the fourth.

They four snakes swam and snapped at Lev and Ezra. Lev held his ground, showing no fear. "The Enchantress is here? Where is she?"

"The Graveyard holds both bot and man," said the first snake.

"To rescue them she has a plan," said snake three, nipping as she swam by.

"A witch has cards and tricks and games," the second sang.

"To get Green Beard to say his name," said the fourth.

"What are they talking about?" Ezra asked.

"If anyone says the true name of an undead pirate, the name given to his or her at birth, they'll die if they fall in the water," Lev explained.

Ezra looked skeptical. "How do you ever get a pirate to tell you that?"

"I don't know," admitted Lev, "but if anyone can do it, Madame Haaf can."

The larger of the snakes moved closer to Lev.

"Our lady sends a message. Do not alter.

After calling their name, sends pirates into the water.

Call your army, call your friends.

Drag them to the ocean depths."

Lev agreed, "I will make sure we are ready. What about Grogan and Brody? How do we get them out?"

The second snake pushed her way between Lev and Ezra, attempting to knock them off of the surfboard.

"While Madame tricks the Beard of Green,
Go to the Graveyard sight unseen,
The man of flesh and man of steel,
Are tied up, hidden near the keel.
When she finds the list of names,
They will appear the magic way,
Call the pirate, her or him,
Then take them for a deadly swim."

Lev didn't wait to answer the snake. Instead, he dug his toes into the surfboard conduits and thought of Astro. He held Ezra tight and they were off. Maurea and Bat followed them. When Lev and Ezra came into view of Astro and the villagers, a cheer in the form of dozens of bubbles erupted from the small but mighty group.

Elias and the dolphins swam circles around the boy prince. Astro spun his roller feet as they propelled him to Lev. The two hugged. "I thought maybe you got lost," Astro teased.

"Just testing out the new board," Lev said with a laugh.

Astro nodded towards the snakes. "What did they want?"

"They brought word from Madame Haaf. She's aboard the Graveyard with plans to trick Green Beard into saying his own name."

"Good luck with that," Astro replied, doubtfully. "Any word on Grogan and my brother?"

"Yes, they're being held near the keel."

"Under the water?" Astro gasped, thinking of Grogan.

"I get the impression they're just above it," Lev replied.

"Well, what are we waiting for?" Astro said, starting to move but Lev pulled the bot to a halt.

"Hang on. We can't fight pirates, rescue Grogan and Brody and defeat Green Beard all at once. I have a plan."

"You do?" Astro asked.

"If Alice can find her way in Wonderland maybe I can find mine in Meridium."

"What?"

"Never mind. Gather everyone together. With a little bit of luck this might just work."

<u>Sixteen</u>

"Okay does everyone know what they're supposed to do?" Lev asked after explaining his plan to the rabble group of robot, dolphins and merfolk. Everyone nodded. Astro beamed at him like a proud parent. Ezra and Maurea took their station with Bat who chirped in agreement. "Good. Let's get into position and hope that Madame Haaf has magic on her side."

Inside the Graveyard, Brody twisted his one good arm in its ropes. He cursed, "If my other arm hadn't been broken in the shark fight, I could have gotten us out of here by now."

Grogan sighed. "It's alright, my friend. You did all you could to protect the boy. It will be worth all of the trouble if he makes it to his father in Meridium."

"Hmm," Brody snorted.

"You don't agree that a young boy like that needs his family?" Grogan asked.

"I believe that family can be defined as those who love you and would risk everything for you. And you for them. King Milos is just as bad as Queen Eliza," Brody declared.

"Bold words outside of your programming," Grogan argued.

"I would think you of all people would understand how much Leviathan means to me. Did I not prove it on the beach of Nautilus all those years ago?" Brody whispered.

Grogan was silent for a long time. There was only the sound of Grogan's breathing and Brody's steam engine purring in the tiny keel compartment.

Finally, Grogan said in a much kinder voice. "So it's true. There were signs of it when I found you. And there were the rumors that Madame Haaf had given you a gift to help Anna."

"It's true. I don't remember anything from before that night. Not really. The wind was on Green Beard's side as night fell. That I do remember. Elias and the pod were accompanying us but it was slow going. She was carrying the infant and swimming. She was human despite Madame's gift of gills. When Anna grew too tired to swim any farther, I carried them both. I was faster than her but still we had to be careful. Sometime after the moon was high, directly over the sea, we spotted the shore. Elias said it was too dangerous to move Anna and Lev but I was worried for them both. Anna was so exhausted from her escape. King Milos had chased us, then Green Beard. They both wanted the boy but for different reasons.

I decided that it was worth the risk and carried Anna and Lev, tucked in Anna's cloak through the water, swimming hard. We were nearly to the shore of Nautilus Castle when a harpoon was shot from the starboard bow of the Graveyard," Brody explained.

"That's the one that hit Anna," Grogan whispered, choking on his words.

"No. I thought it hit her. There was so much blood. I was afraid of sharks. Somehow Elias and the pod carried the three of us as far as the bay would allow. When we parted, they formed a barrier line to hold off any predators. I carried Anna to shore and desperately opened the cloak where she had Lev cradled next to her chest. She wasn't breathing. The harpoon and pierced Leviathan's leg. He had lost too much blood for any infant to endure and he had endured a lot in those twenty-four hours. He was barely alive. That's when I made my decision."

"Or maybe my programming made it for you…"Grogan said. He sounded regretful.

"It was my choice," Brody reassured him. "Madame Haaf had given me the last living breath of a fishermen whom she could not save when she was a doctor in the kingdom. It was her one way to save the life of her friend and infant since she could not go with us. But she gave me the choice. I could keep the breath for myself and remain half robot, half human or I could give it as a gift as she had given it to me."

"Do you remember what it felt like?" Grogan asked, twisting his body in his ropes.

"No," said Brody. "I'm glad I don't remember that part, the before part. I only remember that Leviathan opened his very big eyes and stared up me. I had gotten him to the safety of shore. I had to finish the job. So I breathed my only breath into Lev's lungs, passing the extra spark of life from myself to him. He instantly began to cry and from what I knew of humans, I knew that was a good thing. I stepped back in that moment. Madame Haaf had warned me of the effects of magic leaving a body. Any. Body. I don't remember anything after that."

"I'm sorry, Brody. I can see now that Leviathan is like a son to you. I'm an old man full of regrets. Perhaps I should not have sent him to King Milos after all."

"I'll get him back," Brody vowed.

"You? Against a king?" Grogan asked.

"A father will give anything to save his child." Brody looked fiercely at the old man and Grogan knew that it was true. Brody would give a thousand breaths and explode on a thousand shores to make sure Leviathan was safe and happy.

"If we ever get out of here, we'll go together. I have a few things I'd like to say to King Milos as well," Grogan declared.

Suddenly light poured into the cramped keel compartment as Astro yanked open the door. Lev put his finger to his lips then whispered, "You two aren't going to defeat Milos without me, are you?" He gave a little laugh and threw his arms around Brody. Brody's shutters scanned Lev for injuries. The robot pushed the green and blue hair from Lev's face. "What's happening? Are you alright?"

"I'm fine." Lev noticed Brody's missing arm. "Better than you," he teased slightly. "We're working with Madame Haaf," he whispered. Lev turned to Grogan who wore a look of shock. "I'll explain it all later. Come on, let's get out of here."

The three poked their heads out of the end compartment of the Graveyard ship. Grunt was still punching his way through living and skeleton pirates. Slice had given up on using his scalpels to fight and instead had been cutting up the sails and ropes of the ship. "That's one way to keep them from sailing off," Grogan whispered.

Lev gasped. He saw Peck lay, unmoving on the upper deck. He wanted so much to run and take her with them but he had to wait for Madame Haaf's signal. What was she doing?

Meanwhile, in the Graveyard's Captain quarters, Madame Haaf and Green Beard sat across from one another at a splintered, wooden table. A delicate crystal glass shimmered near the witch's hand. She took out a small bottle of potion from her bag and poured it in. She took a long drink. "Where are my manners? Would you like a glass as well?" The Enchantress offered.

"I won't be drinkin' a drop of anything you give me. I'm not falling for one of your spells. Give me the boy and I might not roast your snakes for my supper tonight," Green Beard growled.

"And I am not afraid of you, mangy pirate. Give me the maker of metal men and his minion and I may not send rough seas to break this ship in two," Madame Haaf replied, calmly.

"So it seems you have something that I want and I have something you want," Green Beard said.

"So it would seem," said the witch.

The door to the cabin flung open and Razor drew his sword. "I'll slice her in two!"

Madame glared at him with her yellow, reptile eyes. With a flick of her hand, Razor's sword went flying across the room. The tip of the blade embedded in the wood just above Green Beard's bed. "So nice of you to join our little soiree, Razor. Please, join us," Madame said with a toothy grin. "We were just discussing how to resolve our little problem. I think I have the perfect solution."

"And that is?" Green Beard asked.

"We play for it." The Enchantress held out her hand and a deck of cards shimmered into view.

Green Beard and Razor roared with laughter. Green Beard leaned forward and said, "You dare come aboard my ship and challenge me to a game of cards? You're crazier than I thought. Pirates are the best card players in the whole world!" He laughed some more. Catching his breath he spoke in a wheeze, "Ok so WHEN I win, you give me the boy and never cross my path again."

Madame began to shuffle her cards. "And WHEN I win, you will tell me your real name."

Both Razor and Green Beard stopped laughing and stared at Madame. "That goes against the pirate code," argued Razor, dead serious and quiet.

"I am no pirate," Madame Haaf answered. "You see, I know that there is a treasure hidden somewhere in this room. It is protected by a spell. I could smell the black magic the minute I came aboard but it stinks the most in here."

"That's just the Captain's boots," Razor lied.

"Silence!" Madame yelled.

"If you win, I will give you the Prince, son of Milos, to ransom to his royal father. You will be the richest pirate who ever sailed the seven seas," Madame said. As she spoke the words, she painted a picture in Green Beard's mind. In the vision, the Captain was standing at the helm wearing a new hat with a giant peacock feather and a blazing red velvet jacket with coattails that danced in the wind.

"And if you win?" Razor asked, unaffected by the enchantment.

"If I win, the Captain here just has to say a few tiny words. He must say the name his mother gave him when he was born. This is a bargain."

Razor snapped his giant jaws to bring Green Beard back from his daydream. The Captain blinked.

"So we have a deal?"

"It's a bet," Green Beard agreed. He wiped the puce, yellow green snot from his nose and mustache with his hand and held it out to shake to seal the contract. Even Razor gagged at the idea of squeezing a hand full of snot. He'd seen a pirate's contract before but he never got used to it.

Madame Haaf did not shy away from the vulgar, mucus filled hand. Instead, she leaned her body over the table to take his hand in hers, ensuring her snout and jagged teeth were nearly touching his face. The two advisories stared at one another, neither willing to break eye contact for the longest time. Finally, the enchantress sat back down in her chair and shuffled the cards once more.

"What shall it be?" Green Beard asked. "Wist?"

"That game is for officers. You serve no king or queen here," Madame informed him.

"War?" Green Beard suggested.

"That takes too long," Madame protested. "How about a real pirate's game?" She did a card trick and a fancy shuffle and said, "Let's play Davey Jones' Locker."

Green Beard turned pale with fear, but Razor looked confused. "What's that?"

"And you call yourself a real pirate?" Madame clicked her tongue. "The game was invented by pirates and therefore it is simple. We each draw a card, taking turns, trying to reach a total of thirty but no more. No more than thirty! The first one who makes it closest to third but not over, wins."

"Why, there's nothing to that, Captain!" Razor patted Green Beard on the back.

"There's just one little thing she forgot to mention," Green Beard said, gravely.

"What do ya mean?" Razor asked.

"Ah yes," Madame confessed. "There is one tiny exception to the rule. If either player draws a number five, then it's straight to Davey Jones Locker. They lose!"

Madame Haaf's sea snakes shimmered into view; two wrapping themselves lovingly around her neck like a shawl and the other two swam around Green Beard's head, snapping and nipping at his giant hat. He swatted at them and one gave him a good bite on the wrist.

Razor leapt from his chair, nearly knocking over the table to defend his Captain. His giant jaws snapped the snakes and his double rows of shark teeth threatened to eat one of them whole if they got close enough.

"Call off your dogs!" Green Beard shouted, nursing his bleeding wrist. He glanced sideways at Razor. The giant shark's eyes were completely black as he fought the urge to take a bite out of Green Beard. The smell of blood in the water was delicious to his heightened senses. "And you," Green Beard shouted, "get out of here before I run you through with my sword."

Razor gritted his teeth in restraint. He considered just eating one of the snakes in the very instance to calm his craving. He looked at Madame Haaf and decided he'd better not. Instead, he roared in anger at all of them and stormed out of the room.

Shouts erupted on deck as Razor took his wrath out on whom ever crossed his path. The witch hoped that she had bought Leviathan enough time to rescue Brody and Grogan without the threat of Razor near the keel. Now, she needed the shark out of the room. Green Beard could fall under her charms but Razor could not. She needed Green Beard alone if she was to win the game. It all came down to the game.

"Shall we begin?" Madame asked. She drew the first card.

Seventeen

Lev, Brody and Grogan hid behind several barrels on deck watching the sword fighting between the pirates and the robots. A few of Grogan's spider bots were still stinging the living pirates. "Why don't they fall asleep like the guards in the castle?" Lev asked.

"Pirates are harder to weaken," Grogan whispered. "They've been through storms, survived giant waves, fought in dozens of sword fights, been attacked by island natives and likely nearly starved a time or two. Being a pirate isn't for the faint of heart."

Slice was back using his tail and it's selection of knives in place of a sword. He knocked one human pirate overboard. Lev wanted to stand up and cheer but it wasn't a good idea considering that would give away their position. He could hear clicks and chirps from the side of the water where the pirate fell into the ocean.

Through a small break in the wood, Lev peeked through to see Elias sounding his alarm. A skeleton wearing the same hat and boots as the once living pirate was climbing up one of the ropes dangling off of the ship. Brody took a turn looking through the crack in the wooden ship. He leaned back into the shadows with exhaustion. "How do you fight something that can't be killed?"

"Ezra just asked me the same question," Lev laughed.

"Who?" Brody asked.

Lev just blushed.

"Oh it can be killed, but no blade will bring an end to a skeleton crew," Grogan sighed.

"Come on, Madame Haaf," Lev whispered. "Hurry up."

Meanwhile, in the Captain's quarters of the Graveyard, Madame Haaf played the card she drew from the pile, "two of spades."

Green Beard laughed. "Ye won't be reachin' thirty any time soon with numbers like that." The witch ignored him and gestured for him to take his turn. Green Beard stood up and walked across the room to a cabinet. He took out a tin mug and filled it with cool water and returned to the table. He took a long drink. The water ran down the green snot of his beard and dripped on to his lap.

When he returned, his large hand reached across the table and drew a card. He looked at it and grinned. His yellow teeth exaggerated his disgusting smile. "King of hearts," he declared and set the card down with enthusiasm. "See, that's how ya get to thirty in no time." Madame just smiled and nodded.

The sea snakes nuzzled their mistress as she reached for another card. She stopped. "You know, you are doing so well. Why not add to our little agreement?"

"What did you have in mind?" Green Beard sneered.

"If you win, I will give you the boy prince to ransom off to King Milos AND to sweeten the deal, I will add the services of my sea snakes."

"What do I need 'em for?"

"Once you have ransomed the boy to the King of the sea, my lovelies will re-capture the boy so that you may ransom him again to Queen Eliza and King James." The witch leaned in and sent her charms across the table as she said, "You could double your fortune."

Green Beard wore a dreamy look on his face as he imagined a cave, then an entire island full of treasure. He blinked sleepily at Madame Haaf. Then, he shook his head to clear his mind. "Uh, so say that I agree to increasing our bet. What if YOU win?"

"If I win, I require just a small token, really. I will need your name at birth AND the names of all of your crew. I know you must have that written down somewhere here in this cabin. Any good captain would, just incase."

Madame Haaf watched the eyes of Green Beard. As he considered the offer, he looked towards the cabinet where he had poured himself a mug of water. Without saying a word, he had given the location of the names away. She smiled at the pirate. "Do we have a deal?"

She sent more charms, more visions of gold, rubies, sapphires and pearls. Green Beard smiled with heavy eyes and agreed. The witch reached out and drew the next card off the top of the pile. Green Beard laughed greedily under his breath as she slowly turned it over and placed it next to first card. "The ten of hearts," she declared. "Were you hoping I would draw a five?"

"That treasure is as good as mine. I've got luck on my side. If you're a gracious loser, I may even let you swim back to that wreck at the bottom of the ocean," the pirate gloated.

"How generous. But please don't be rude. The Dream is my home," Madame scolded. "You're draw, Captain."

Green Beard wiped his runny nose and then reached for a card. "Sounds more like a nightmare," he said under his breath. He flipped the card over with confidence, staring the enchantress directly in the eye as he did so. After a moment, they both looked at the card. The Captain exhaled in relief, "A nine of clubs. Ha! I'm still ahead of you!"

Green Beard jumped up from his chair and began to dance around the table chanting, "Who's the richest pirate on the sea ? Green Beard! Green Beard! Do you know the pirate? Yep it's me! Green Beard! Green Beard!"

Madame Haaf whispered something to her sea snakes. The two around her neck slowly shimmered into nothing, disappearing into the shadows. Meanwhile, she drummed her painted, clawed fingernails on the table and patiently waited.

After a while, she cleared her throat and asked, "Are you quite finished?" Green Beard stopped his dancing and cleared his throat. He coughed up something slimy and spit it out on the floor. Madame Haaf sneered in disgust. It was time to draw again.

The Enchantress had twelve and Green Beard had nineteen. The game was inching closer to one of them reaching thirty. Madame's yellow eyes searched the shadows of the room. Translucent shimmers swirled around the captain's cabinet and she smirked just a bit. Her pets had found something and were working their limited magic on the lock. She had to keep the wretched pirate distracted.

The witch reached over and drew a card while humming a tune. Green Beard cocked his head to one side. "I know that tune," he said. He sang along for a moment,

"The good man he came home one night, the good man home came he.

There he spied an old saddle horse where no horse should there be.

It's a cow, it's a cow cried the good man's wife.

A cow, just a cow can't ya see.

Far I've ridden and much I've seen, a saddle on a cow there's never been."

Green Beard was enjoying himself and his expression said that he was feeling very lucky in the match. The Enchantress's scaly hand picked the top card from the deck and turned it over. It was her turn to laugh. "Ten of diamonds. You know, those diamonds are a girl's best friend. That makes twenty-two for me. Beat that!"

Green Beard stopped singing and flew into a rage. "You think just because you drew the card of jewels that means you're going to win the treasure?! Well, you're wrong! That treasure is as good as mine! Mine I tell ya!"

Under all the commotion of his yelling and shouting, Madame Haaf heard the gentle click of a lock popping open. She gave a sideways glance of approval to the two shimmering snakes who had returned to the shadows of the room, one of them with a scroll in its mouth. She flashed her pets the ever so slightest of smiles and nodded towards the door. The two took their prize as they slipped out of the Captain's quarters.

Meanwhile, Lev, Brody and Grogan watched helplessly as their robot friends were nearly finished. Slice was dueling a living pirate who was being bitten by one of Grogan's spiders. His scalpels, once a blur like a tornado or steel and metal bike chains now was slowing as his steam power ran low. One of Slice's knives connected with the pirate's hand. The man merely laughed. Instead of running away in pain, he used his scabbard and aimed for Slice's underbody. The Kismet's robotic doctor lost several cogs and fell. It took all of his strength to slither quickly to a porthole and take shelter in the ocean.

That left Grunt, Peck and a few remaining spiders to fight. "There must be something we can do," Brody said, desperately. Grogan tensed as Razor nearly broke the wheel of the ship fighting the first two of Madame Haaf's sea snakes. The shark lunged, first with his sword and then with his huge jaws. The snakes swirled around the shark's dorsal fin, taking bites out of it when they dared and trying to dodge the blade and many rows or jagged teeth that threatened to devour them whole if they made one false move.

Leviathan looked to Green Beard's door and saw it move ever so slightly. He squinted, trying to make out the strange shimmering and the floating of an object. He watched as it darted from shadow to shadow in the commotion of the deck until it nearly reached the trio of onlookers.

'Make some room,
To share our news.

To save the day,
Just say these names.
Then one by one you toss and flip,
Into the sea from Graveyard ship," sang the two serpents. Lev breathed a sigh of relief. He never thought he'd be happy to see them but he was elated.

"What's this?" Grogan asked as the first snake dropped a scroll to the floor. It opened and he began to read the words. A nearby pirate who had stood off to the side to watched the fight stopped laughing and froze at the sound of his own name, his REAL name being spoken. He looked around in fright. The second snake saw her chance and slithered like a torpedo, colliding with the man's boots. He was knocked back, lost his balance and fell overboard into the ocean.

Ezra and several farmers were waiting. Everyone watched as the pirate transformed into a skeleton when his body tumbled into the water. The farmers fought the skeleton in the water and soon, Ezra returned to the surface to announce their victory.

It gave Lev an idea. "Grogan, gather as many of the crew as you can. Brody, help who ever is left to take their fights to the edges of the deck."

"You're giving the orders now?" Grogan thundered. Lev gave Grogan a look of confidence as he stood, unwavering. A large grin spread across the man's face. "Maybe you're a prince after all, eh?"

"Or maybe someone just showed me what it is to have courage," Lev replied giving a nod to

Brody. "Now let's go while we still have surprise on our side."

"Where are you going, young master?" Brody asked, protectively.

Lev gave Brody a mischievous look that the robot had never seen before. "I've got a wave to ride!" He ran to the side and jumped into the water, swimming to Ezrea and Maurea. "Ladies, are we ready to swim with the pirates?"

Ezra gave him a wink and handed Lev his steam-powered surfboard. All four sea snakes slithered to the side and looked overboard to Lev. They sang in chorus:

"We are wishing,
For pirate fishing,
But beware of waters dark,
Razor has gone to gather sharks."

Lev gulped back fear. He searched the deck and cursed to himself. Razor had slipped away! He pushed the thought aside. There was nothing he could do about it. "Then we had better hurry and rid this ship of every pirate we can as fast as we can. Call out some names!"

And so, the unlikely band of robots, merpeople, sea snakes and humans fought the pirates on their home ship. The sea snakes read off the names that the pirates had hoped they would never hear again in their lives. Grunt, Peck, Astro and Brody fought with blades, barrels and their own bodies to push the vulnerable pirates to the ship's edge. Lev rode his board around the Graveyard, leaping up on the tops of waves and grabbing pirates by their coats, boots (and even a long beard in one case). Once the doomed pirates fell into the water, the kelp farmers and Maurea took care of the rest.

Peck gave a cheer despite her injured wing when the last pirate had fallen, and the deck was cleared. The rest of Leviathan's friends cheered as well. The robotic spiders scurried across the deck and huddled together as if reuniting in a happy dance.

But their luck was short lived. Ezra called out to Lev as a huge, dark wave was approaching from the south.

"Razor," Lev sighed. "Everyone in the water, get to your boats and take shelter in the Kismet. Razor and his sharks are coming!"

Lev landed his board on the surface of the water. He took Ezra quickly to Bat. There he made sure she was safely in the cockpit. "Go to the Kismet with Bat," he told Ezra.

"What about you?" Bat chirped.

"Madame Haaf hasn't returned yet. None of us are safe while Green Beard and Razor are causing trouble. Can you two make sure that the farmers and their families make it to the Kismet? They'll be safe there from Razor and his thugs there."

Ezra gave him a worried smile that made his heart beat a little faster. He touched the medallions around his neck. In that moment, he took the one that had been Grogan's and placed it over Ezra's head. It shined ever so slightly in the water. She gripped the seal of the Kraken and opened her mouth to protest but Lev gave her hand a quick squeeze and then he was off on his board, powering up to the surface.

<u>Eighteen</u>

Madame Haaf could hear the cries growing louder by the minute, as she knew it would. Green Beard had no idea that he was the only pirate who remained onboard, thanks to her thieving snakes. Nor did he know a squad of sharks, led by Razor was on its way to attack the resistance fighters lead by Lev and Astro. The Enchantress and the Captain stared across the table from one another. "Your turn, Captain," she said.

Green Beard stroked the green mucus in his beard and stared at the deck of cards. Finally, he held his breath as he reached out and pulled the top card from the pile. He exhaled and flipped it over; a four of diamonds. "Seems the jewels be likin' me too," he declared. "The score is twenty two to twenty-three and I'm in the lead."

"Your luck is with you. Would you care to raise the stakes again?" Madame asked.

"What more could you possibly want besides my real name and the names of my crew? What's left?" Green Beard argued.

The Enchantress looked innocent and menacing all at the same time. "If I win," she said, "I become the Captain of the Graveyard."

At this, Green Beard roared with laughter. He gripped his belly and had to push his chair back away from the table as his other fist pounded on it's wooden planks. A few tears flowed down his cheeks, he laughed so hard. It took a whole minute of gasping for air until all that remained was a huge smile. "And who, by chance is gonna sail it? You'd be doomed before you even raised a sail."

"Why is that?" Madame asked.

"Every pirate knows that it's bad luck to have a woman onboard," Green Beard declared.

"That's for me to worry about," the Enchantress shrugged.

"And if I win?" Green Beard asked, hungry with greed.

"I will make you a potion," she answered.

Green Beard looked serious, considering the deal. "What kind of potion?"

"Whatever you like. Would you like to be young again? Or maybe a love potion?"

Green Beard wrinkled his nose. "What good is any of that?"

"Something else then, perhaps?"

Green Beard thought hard and as he did so, Madame Haaf tapped her fingers once again. She sent her charm across the table and planted an idea in the Captain's head. Within moments, Green Beard had an idea come to him. "I wish to be the most feared Pirate on the Seven Seas."

"Why Captain," Madame said candidly, "that is what your first mate, Razor is for, is it not?"

Green Beard shrugged, "With a potion like that, I wouldn't need a first mate. I could keep the Graveyard running all on me own."

"You are a clever man," Madame said charmingly. "Ok. If you win, you get a fear potion added to our deal. And if I win, the Graveyard is mine."

"Agreed," puffed Green Beard, impatiently, "now draw!"

Madame slowly reached her claw across the table and drew a card. She did not hold her breath or wait to reveal its face like her competitor. Instead, she turned it over and said with a sly grin, "Seven of spades. That makes twenty-nine for me. I am very close to thirty, am I not?"

"It ain't over til I says it's over," Green Beard growled and quickly snatched a card from the deck. Madam smirked as she watched the pirate's face. It went from being as white as a ghost to as red and hot as oven. He began shaking with rage and Madame Haaf snatched the card from his hand and placed it down on his side of the table.

The two of them stared down at the dreaded number five card. The witch bared her crocodile teeth and declared, "Number five, Captain Green Beard. You lose and I win."

"I'll never give you anything. I will throw you in the sea before I tell you my name or give you my ship!" Green Beard declared at the top of his lungs. "My crew will defend me. All you have are your pathetic little worms to save you."

The door opened casually and in walked Grogan and Leviathan. "I think you had better check on your ship, Captain. I don't see any crew left," Leviathan informed him.

Green Beard roared but was soon silenced as Madame summoned a chair from the corner and sent it flying so hard into the pirate's knees that he was forced to sit down. The four sea snakes erupted from the shadows in the room and wrapped themselves around Green Beard like tight ropes. Whenever the Captain tried to struggle, they bit him in the knees and elbow, making the man yelp.

"I think he called us little worms," said the first.

"I think it's his time to squirm," said the second.

"Only one more thing remains," said the third.

"You must say your given name," declared the fourth.

"I won't!" Green Beard cried. "You can't make me."

"True," said Madame Haaf. "But I can curse you. I am a witch, after all."

Green Beard gulped back fear. His two choices were to say his real name and know that he would drown if he fell into the ocean or take his chances and live with whatever evil curse Madame Haaf put on him. He sniffed as he considered the two options.

From somewhere below the ship, a boom erupted. Green Beard and the snakes fell sideways to the floor. The others had to grab on to the nearest piece of the ship to steady themselves.

"Cannons?" Grunt asked as he stumbled on the deck towards Lev.

Lev heard them first. The rogue sharks who gave their alliance to Razor had arrived in a wave of teeth and fins. "Razor's battering the ship from under," Lev told Grogan.

"They're going to destroy the ship," said Brody, coming down from the crow's nest.

Madame Haaf moved with purpose, swiping Green Beard's swashbuckling hat off floor. "No they're not! It's my ship now! Grogan, call all of your metal creatures together."

"And why should we help you and your ship?" Grogan asked, folding his arms in protest.

"Razor has not only gathered his sharks. Captain Calico and the might of King Milos has joined them. If the boy is to survive this, it will take every one of us."

<u>Nineteen</u>

Lev made trips taking Grogan and Brody back to the Kismet on his board where they could regroup with Maurea, Ezra, Slice, the remaining service bots, and the farmers.

Grogan took the tube from the ceiling and made an announcement over the intercom of the submarine. "This is Grogan, all hands to the Pool Room. On the double."

Brody pulled Lev aside. "Follow me," the robot insisted. Lev hated to be away from the others, but he did as his old friend requested. When they entered Lev's old room, Slice was there. The serpent-bot looked a bit battered, but he nodded to Brody when he and Lev walked in.

"Can you replace Brody's arm?" Leviathan asked the medic.

Slice looked confused and looked to Brody for an answer.

"There's no time for that now Leviathan," Brody explained. "A boy with a heart of gold is no match for a bunch of bloodthirsty sharks." Brody turned to slice and gave a nod.

As Slice worked on Brody's chest plate, the bodyguard explained, "Do you remember when I said Slice had done some repairs to my chest plate the first night you arrived?"

"Yes," Lev answered. That first night on the Kismet seemed so far away when he thought about it.

"Well, Slice here just put a second layer on. Two is better than one, right?"

"Right," Agreed Lev.

"But two on me is no good when you're made of flesh and bones and we're heading into a fight, Leviathan." Brody's shiny breast plate fell to the floor and Lev looked on as his best friend's beat up and dull body remained. "A Prince needs armor if he's going into battle."

Slice moved again in a blur of knives and scalpels, sharp enough to cut through steel. Brody put an arm protectively in front of Lev until the serpentine medic was finished. Slice looked up from the small cart where he worked. "It isn't polished or royal, but it will keep any shark bite from reaching your skin." Slice held up pieces to a suit of armor.

"But—Brody," Lev protested.

"No arguing, Leviathan. I can't stop you from entering the fight. You've grown up too much now to stay inside the Kismet. I know that now. But I can protect you this way. It's what I was built for."

Lev opened his mouth to protest. Brody looked so vulnerable without his second layer. But Brody insisted. "It's what your mother and Grogan would want."

Leviathan shut his mouth and held his arms out to Slice. "Show me how to put it on."

Slice smiled at Brody and the two began to help Lev suit up. Slice explained, "The helmet I made from a spare cooking pot. Don't tell Peck. The shoulder and shirt plates are made from Brody's second layer and held together by wires to make it flexible at all your jointed parts. I have cut the neck plate out and made protectors for your knees instead."

Brody added, "You would not be able to breathe underwater if your gills were covered."

"Got it," Lev agreed.

"These are chain mail gloves that Grogan once used while diving. They'll slow you down when you swim, but they'll help you if you get into a fight in the water. Your feet I've left free. You'll need to make direct skin-to-board contact in order for the board to go where you want it to go. You will also need the webbing on your feet to swim. Be careful. Your feet are now your most vulnerable part of you."

Lev nodded.

"Now, time to see if any of the bots need modifications before they set out," said Slice. He was gone before Lev to thank him.

Instead, he turned to Brody. There were a million things he wanted to say and a thousand stories he wanted to share since the last fight with the sharks and Razor. He knew there was no time for any of it. Instead, Lev let his eyes fill with the tears he'd felt since the minute he saw Brody in the keel compartment, and he jumped into the robots arms and hugged him. Brody held Lev tight. "Thank you, Brody," Lev whispered. "Thank you for everything."

Lev looked up to Brody with a tear streaked face. Brody tousled Lev's hair like he did back in Nautilus Castle. "It has been my honor and my privilege. Now stay close and let's show those sharks who really rules the sea."

Lev and Brody made their way to the Pool Room and joined the others. Grogan and Maurea were missing. Lev found Ezra in the ocean pool. "Where's your mother and Grogan?"

"My mother said she had an idea and the two of them left," Ezra explained.

Astro heard them and added, "They went to the docking bay. I have no idea why. All that's left there are the wind walkers, which are useless under water and the elephant and rhino bots, which I'm pretty sure would sink."

"The elephant and rhino made it back from the siege on the castle?" Lev asked in surprise.

"No," Astro explained. "Grogan always makes two of everything." Then Astro looked Lev up and down and gave Brody a sideways look. "Seems I missed the memo on dressing alike."

"You're just jealous you can't pull off the battered metal look like I can," Brody teased.

Lev rolled his eyes.

Grogan returned with Maurea in his arms. They were in a hurry but they both seemed pleased. Grogan had that will look in his eyes and his goggles were riding on the top of his head. "Ok everybody, with the Prince's permission I'd like to invite everyone to go fishing."

<u>Twenty</u>

"Fishing?" Lev asked.

Grogan nodded. "Prince Leviathan, how do you catch a fish?"

Lev shrugged, "With a line and a hook?"

Grogan set Maurea back in the pool and then turned to the farmers at the water's edge, "Ladies and gentle-mer, how do you catch a school of fish?"

One woman shrugged, "With bubbles, of course. We trap them in bubbles just like the dolphins do."

"Exactly," Grogan clapped his hands with enthusiasm. "With the help of our friend Elias, that's exactly what we're going to do. And then, we are going to become the most feared fish in all the sea, thanks to the brilliance of Maurea and a few minor enhancements on some old robotic friends."

Lev leaned over to Ezra and whispered, "How do you make that many bubbles at once to catch a whole school of fish?"

Ezra shrugged, "For a prince of the sea, you sure have a lot to learn. We sing, of course."

On the Graveyard, Madame Haaf was performing an enchantment on the deck. Grunt carried barrel after barrel down into the hull in the hopes that it might make it more difficult for Razor and the sharks to burst through.

Peck flew from one corner to the other, directing Grunt as to where to set each barrel. "It will be a shame if all those apples end up in the ocean," she sighed. Grunt turned around to place another barrel but when he went to set it down, the ship was gone. He fell backwards in shock. All he could see was water.

"Grunt is walking on water? Grunt does not think this possible," he said in disbelief.

"I've enchanted it, you metal bucket of bolts!" Madame Haaf shouted. "If it works on you lot, let's hope it works on those fish! She wasn't sure since none of her spells had worked on Razor when she and Green Beard were playing cards. It was a risk she would have to take."

Grunt crawled to the top deck, feeling his way along while Peck flew over the area, searching for the Graveyard. "It looks like you two are just floating on air! Look at the Captain!"

Green Beard was still being held to the chair by the sea snakes. He looked far more frightened when he couldn't find a nice secure floor for his feet. "Give me back my ship!" Green Beard bellowed.

"It's my ship! I won it fair and square and soon I will have your name too," replied the witch.

"Never! I'll rot in this chair before I tell you my name!" Green Beard shouted.

"That, my dear Captain can be arranged," Madame cooed.

Lev stared wide eyed at the place where he'd left the Graveyard as he approached from his surfboard. He called up to the Enchantress, "Permission to come…aboard or err, afloat like you or…I don't know. Where is the Graveyard exactly?"

"It's here, I've just charmed it into invisibility for the moment," Madame Haaf said as he leaned over the side and spoke to Lev.

"Grogan and Maurea have a plan. Can you hold off Razor if he tries to come aboard?"

"I can handle one little sardine like him, of course," she said confidently.

"I don't suppose you could make a cage or something once we catch them all?" Lev asked.

"Nothing gonna hold all them sardines, my Prince," Madame laughed.

"Right, well, we'll just have to hope that plan A works. Grunt, come with me. We can use your help." Grunt jumped into the water without hesitation. Lev smiled at the witch, "Wish me luck." He guided his surfboard away from the invisible Graveyard and plunged into the water. "Here goes nothing," he said to himself.

As his body transformed, he saw Brody and Astro filling Grunt in on the plan. The three robots swam slightly behind and on either side of Leviathan. The team swam headlong into the shiver. At first, the swarming sharks were so busy trying to ram the hull they could no longer see but still detected with their other senses, they didn't even notice Lev. It was Razor who spotted Lev first.

"The prince!" Razor shouted.

"Come on," Lev whispered. "Take the bait, take the bait."

The entire shiver turned and dove, heading right for Lev. "Let's go!" Astro called out.

Lev led the robots and the sharks away from the Graveyard. Brody reported to Grogan, "So far, so good. We're almost in position."

The sharks were gaining on them. From behind, Lev heard a fight between one of Razor's gang and Grunt.

"Ezra, get ready!" Lev shouted, sending his signal ahead of him, hoping his bubbled message reached her in time.

The team arrived at their mark and the sharks swarmed them, threatening to overtake them in minutes. Lev felt Brody immediately by his side. He handed Lev a sword from one of the long gone crew of Graveyard. "When we get back to the Kismet, the first thing I'm teaching you is swordsmanship."

"And I'm teaching you some new dance moves," Astro teased. "You've caught the eye of a girl. All girls like a good dancer." A reef shark tried to take a bite out of Astro's arm and then the fight was on.

Brody swiped his sword at a blue shark with his one remaining arm. "Girl?," he asked while fighting. "What girl?"

Astro easily frightened the reef shark but more kept coming. Lev dodged a bite from another blue shark. He swung his sword left and right, pushing the sharks back into position. Grunt had fended off a large shark and joined Lev in pushing back the swarm of giant fins and black, lifeless eyes.

Lev ducked two sharks who tried to attack from different angles. "She's just a friend," Lev argued.

Bubbles began to rise from somewhere in the depths below. "Wait," Brody instructed, and the team held their ground. They had to keep the majority of the sharks in that exact spot. Swimming anywhere else would only draw them away from their mark. "Wait," he said a few seconds later. "The bubble cloud increased, and Lev could hear Elias talking to Ezra from somewhere below them. Soon, there were so many bubbles that Lev couldn't see. He felt a strong metal arm pull him out of the screen of water and trapped air.

"Not you, only sharks," Grunt explained.

"Thank you, Grunt," Lev said.

The robots watched as the sharks became trapped in a thick curtain of bubbles. The shiver couldn't see which way to go, bumping into one another and taking bites at passersby as the curtain tightened.

Lev could hear the mer-song from the farmers and Ezra below. He was tempted to join them. Instead, he mouthed the words. He closed his eyes for just a brief moment and felt a wave of pride. They didn't need to kill the creatures of the sea. But it wouldn't hurt to give them a good scare and send them far away from the Meridium.

Brody watched Lev and nudged him with his one arm, "Just a friend, eh?"

Lev smiled and blushed.

Without warning, it was Lev and the bots who had the scare. Before Lev could understand what was happening, Razor and Captain Calico, a Great White and a Giant Squid were headed straight for them.

Astro, Brody and Grunt formed a tight ring of protection around Lev, but Captain Calico spread out her long tentacles, clamping down on Astro and shaking him. She threw him out to the open sea. Then, she grabbed for Brody and caught his leg.

Brody swam hard against her pull. Eventually, he changed tactics and let her drag him towards her. When he was close enough, he plunged his sword into her soft body. Blood filled the water and the sharks in the bubble net went crazy.

Lev called out for Grogan. He heard the rumble of the machines below but as the boy maneuvered on his board to make it down to lower depths to tell Grogan what was happening, he was stopped dead in the water. As Lev turned, he found himself nose to nose with Razor.

Lev knew he couldn't outfight the immense Shark pirate, nor could he out swim him. The armor on Lev's body suddenly felt very heavy. He just hoped that it would be thick enough to resist the rows and rows of Razor's deadly teeth.

Razor chomped his jaws as if he were smacking his lips. "While Captain Calico's blood does smell delicious, I bet it's not nearly as tasty as yours."

"If you eat me," Lev warned, "you'll have King Milos to answer to."

"Hmm, maybe," Razor laughed. "Or maybe I will just eat the king as well and crown myself king. Just imagine it, no more fighting and searching for gold. No more taking orders from that mucus factory, Green Beard. Instead, everyone will have to listen to me." At that last word, Razor flashed Lev a smile so big, he could smell the rotting fish stuck in the shark's teeth. "What do you think? King Razor. It has a nice ring to it, don't you think?" In the blink of an eye, the giant shark clamped his teeth on Lev's middle. He didn't feel the shark's pointed teeth, but as the metal buckled under the pressure, Lev wondered if his ribs might be crushed. He heard his spine pop. Lev wanted to scream but refused to give Razor any encouragement.

"King Razor sounds like a terrible name," thundered a voice from below, followed by a roar so loud, the water in Lev's gills vibrated.

The curtain of bubbles around the sharks had slowly dissipated and in its place was a vibration so strong that it stunned everything in its path. A huge billow of purple and grey, rose from the depths. As it floated upwards, it grew bigger than a boat, then bigger than a farmhouse, and finally, Lev felt Peck tug at his armor as the little bird bot pulled with all of her might to get the prince to safety. He was still trapped in Razor's jaws.

The monster from the depths grew and with it, a terrible trumpeting sound that traveled through the water. The sharks who had once been caught in the net of bubbled scattered as they watched the beast fifty times their size rise from the fathoms below.

Razor gaped and his jaws opened, releasing Lev just before the boy's body was crushed between the steel plates of armor. Lev was grateful that it saved him from being eaten alive, but he'd definitely need to work on the design, so he was crushed to death next time. He watched Razor dart in one direction then the other in panic. Captain Calico joined him as she screamed, "Swim you fool, it's the Kraken!"

The roar thundered again and said, "I'd know your smell anywhere, Razor. You stole my treasure from King Milos. You stole it and I want it back!"

Razor shook with fright, frozen with fear in the water. Captain Calico abandoned him and swam away as far and fast as her tentacles would take her. The voice boomed again, "I want my treasure!"

"Yes, yes," stumbled Razor. "I'll go get it. I just have to ask the Captain where it is."

"Bring me my treasure!" The voice erupted sending shock waves through the water again. Lev clenched his teeth and again was thankful for Brody's armor.

Razor took off like a torpedo. He swam so absentmindedly that he ran into the invisible Graveyard and screamed. He tried several more times to swim away until he finally cleared the vessel.

Once their enemies had deserted that part of the ocean in exchange for the lives, huge bubbles surfaced at the edge of the Graveyard. Madame Haaf pulled Lev up by the hand. She muttered a few words and the ship reappeared. Lev was thankful for the familiar sensation of solid wood under his feet.

Peck was next to exit the ocean as she flew over the ship, scanning the waves for signs of life. Grogan and Maurea popped their heads up to the surface, an immense purple and grey cloth trailing behind them.

"Where's the elephant and the rhino?" Lev called to them.

"Sunk as soon as Ezra, Elias and the villagers stopped sending up their bubbles of air," Grogan said, but he didn't sound the least bit disappointed about it.

"Hey, we can't just spend our whole day singing while the rest of you have all the fun," Ezra teased and Lev smiled, happy to see her.

"Oh sure, you guys get to be giant land animals while the rest of us were in fierce bot to sword combat," came Brody's voice.

"Speak for yourself, brother, I was just getting started," Astro jabbed at Brody.

"Oh, is that what you were doing when you got flung out into the open ocean?" Brody teased back.

Lev gained back some of his strength and helped his friends on to the deck of the Graveyard. Brody knocked on Lev's chest plate when the two were reunited. "Looks like you'll need a tune up," Brody said, opening and closing his optical shutter in a wink.

"Oh, I don't know, I kind of like it this way. Now it looks more like yours," Lev smiled and hugged Brody.

Maurea called up to Madame Haaf, "The Captain, the Captain has stolen my boat!" Ezra's mother pointed to Green Beard who was putting distance between him and the Graveyard.

Instead of chasing Green Beard with a curse, the witch ran to the Captain's quarters. There, her four beloved sea snakes lay lifeless on the battered floor.

Madame Haaf picked each one up and cradled them in her arms. A crocodile isn't supposed to cry real tears, but the witch did as she rocked her pets back and forth in her leathery arms.

"He was too quick," whispered the first.

"Gave us the slip," coughed the second.

"We are to blame," wheezed the third.

"He gave no name," gasped the fourth.

Madame Haaf rejoiced and sang. "None of that matters as long as you're alive! Just rest my babies. I will take care of you."

"Captain Calico said that Green Beard knows where the treasure is," Lev said.

"Don't you have the map? Are you not a Prince?" The Witch snapped at him.

"Yes," Lev shrugged. "I guess I do have the map."

"Then get to reading it, boy. That map isn't gonna talk to no one else but you," she scolded.

"You forget," Grogan reminded them all, "The Graveyard runs on fear."

"Then I suggested you find a new system of propulsion. Are you not an inventor?" Madame asked.

<u>Twenty-one</u>

Lev stretched the map out on to the table in the Captain's quarters as Madame Haaf, Grogan and Brody looked on. The first set of coordinates shimmered up as if appearing from the water, followed by a picture of a small island. "It says that's where we will find a man who can help us."

"A man isn't treasure," Madame Haaf protested.

"The map only tells me what it wants to tell me," Lev shrugged.

"Hmm. Me and this map are gonna have a talk," the witch griped and headed for the door. "If anybody needs me, I will be below in the sick bay."

"I'll get word to Maurea to set the coordinates on the Kismet," Grogan said, and he headed out on to the deck. Bat chirped and opened her cockpit for the inventor.

Astro jumped in next to him. "I need to make sure the Kismet security defenses are back online. See you tonight for dinner. Oh and I'm teaching you how to line dance. Ezra's coming too. Don't be late," he winked and Grogan laughed.

Brody and Lev were finally alone after what felt like a lifetime of ship repairs and taking in provisions for wherever the map would take them as they searched for the other half of the Kraken's treasure. Lev took the wheel while Brody set the coordinates on Grogan's new navigational invention. Grogan had also converted the Wind Walker into a moving, pivoting group of interdimensional sails, catching every bit of wind and converting it into propulsion. The two friends watched the additional purple and grey sails billow as they caught in the wind off the main mast.

As Lev steered the ship, he asked, "Brody, how old am I really?"

Brody laughed. "You're ten. Madame Haaf was there when you were born and confirmed your birthday."

"Ten," Lev repeated out loud. "Ten is good. Double digits seem about right. I really am growing up."

"Too fast," Brody sighed.

"Can I ask another question?" Lev said, much quieter this time.

"You can ask," Brody said.

"What happened that night on the beach? Madame Haaf said you gave something to me and because of that, it made you explode."

Brody didn't say anything.

After a long while, Lev said, "Brody?"

"I said you could ask," said the bot, "I never said I would answer. "Leviathan was crestfallen. "I will tell you when you're a little bit older," Brody said.

"When I'm eleven?" Lev asked hopefully.

"I will tell you when the time is right; when you need to know," Brody hedged.

"Can I ask another question?" Lev asked, turning the wheel slightly.

"It seems you are incapable of bewilderment. Go ahead," said Brody.

"When will you teach me sword fighting like you promised?"

Quick as a flash, Brody picked Lev up and threw him overboard. The bot dove in after him.

An alarm rang out on deck and Grunt brought the ship to a stop.

"Lesson one. An attack can come at any time and from any direction. Be prepared," Brody grinned.

"That's not really a lesson in sword fighting," Lev argued.

"No, it's a lesson in life. I might now always be here to protect you, Leviathan."

"Yes, you will," Lev said. "I'll make sure of it. I'm the Prince, after all and all my life, I will need a friend like you." They swam, joining Elias for a bit of fun before setting off.

From a league away, Captain Calico and Razor swam as they followed the Kismet. "They've set a course," Razor said. "I'll swim back and let Green Beard know where we're headed." Razor turned in the opposite direction. He added, "Meet me at the rendezvous."

Captain Calico agreed and carefully followed the submarine and ship from a distance. She laughed to herself, "King Milos will be pleased with our progress."

About the Author

Michele Roger is a harpist, writer and teacher. She's also a mother and a grandmother. She grew up speaking French with her grandmother as a child and continued on reading and writing in the language, later writing music for children in French.

Michele is the author of "The Curse of the Snake Princess", "Eternal Kingdom: A Vampire Story," "The Conservatory," several short stories, including "Just Like Dolls," and children's stories "Huggy Muggy Do," and "The Harp and Storm Tamer."

She has also written non-fiction books for adults, including "Contemporary Wedding Ceremonies for the Human Race."

Leviathan Jones and the Sea Witch

<u>Other Books by Michele Roger</u>

The Michigan Macabre Mysteries
Terror Under the Lupin Moon
The Curse of the Snake Princess

and more:

Eternal Kingdom: A Vampire Story
The Harpist
Huggy Muggy Do! (as Michele Roger-
Beresford, with Finnegan Dudley)

www.ingramcontent.com/pod-product-compliance
Lightning Source LLC
Chambersburg PA
CBHW071932190726
48293CB00004B/1246

9 781957 665108